# Come Spy With Me

KT Cavan

Come Spy With Me
By KT Cavan

Published by Asp
An imprint of IndieBooks

ISBN: 978-1-908041-73-9


Set in Times 11/12
Cover design by Jem Butcher
Cover illustration by Jacqueline Bissett

Printed by TJ Books Ltd, Padstow PL28 8RW

# 1

A gentle breeze rustled the curtains and brought the scent of flowers from the garden. Half-asleep, Clemency listened to the *snip-snap* as her mother trimmed back the roses. From the woods by the river came the sleepy, hypnotic call of a wood pigeon, while in the far distance, there was the howl of a jet fighter climbing towards the Bristol Channel.

Everything around her was the same as ever. The shelves of children's books, endlessly re-read, their spines worn to shreds. The piles of toys and games. Her battered hockey stick. Above her, the faint patterns in the plaster of the ceiling that, as a child, she had turned into imaginary lands.

Everything was the same; except her.

These few days at home were driving her insane. Her mind was filled with horrors. A face smashed by a bullet. A man bathed in flames. Another kneeling to be executed. But there was no-one she could tell, not her old school-friends, her parents, not even her brother, and so no way of draining the blackness inside her. Despite this, she dreaded her return to Bern. The work of coding and decoding secret telegrams would be welcome, because it would occupy her mind, but everything else about the city only reminded her of Peter.

Then came the crunch of gravel as a car came up the drive. She frowned. It couldn't be her father. Even having his only daughter home on leave wouldn't bring him back early from the hospital.

She crossed to the window. A dark green Triumph had stopped by the quince tree and a tall, sleek-haired man was standing by the open door, looking around him, taking in the rambling stone house, the immaculate lawn framed by oaks and elms.

Now her mother had appeared from the side of the house, pulling off her gardening gloves. Introductions, explanations, the arrival of their two dogs, Missy so fat these days that her tail seemed to wag her bottom as she waddled forward. Then he was being invited inside, and the embarrassment of the next few minutes could no longer be put off. Clemency slipped on her shoes, checked herself in the mirror, adjusted a strand of hair, and hurried to the top of the stairs just as they entered below.

'There you are, darling,' her mother called up. 'A visitor for you.'

'I'm so sorry to intrude like this, Miss White,' he said. 'I happened to be in the area and it seemed better to speak now rather than wait until Monday.'

'Mr Vaughn's been telling me about how much they think of you at the Office.'

'She's in a lot of demand,' he said smoothly. 'Which is why I'm here. There's the possibility of a short-term secondment and I wanted to snap your daughter up, Mrs White, before it was too late.'

'Yes, I *quite* understand.'

Naturally, her mother considered this a blind, and that his real purpose was to engineer a date with her daughter. Worse, with his Eton confidence and Oxford manners, his youthful maturity – *he's just what Clemency needs, you know* – she'd see Gerald

Vaughn as suitable son-in-law material. What would she think if Clemency told her that he was not in fact a diplomat, but a spy. She could imagine her mother's nose wrinkling a little in distaste.

'I wonder if maybe the dogs need a run,' Vaughn said. 'Then Clemency and I could get our business out of the way.'

'Yes, of course. Why don't you go down to the Mill? There's a beautiful view along the river from there. I'm sure my husband would be happy for me to lend you some wellingtons. You're about the same height.'

'That's so kind of you, Mrs White, but I always have a pair in the car.'

So, for all his city airs, he liked dogs and was at home in the country. Clemency could see her mother ticking the boxes. She hurried off to find her own boots and the leads for the dogs. Only when they had taken the short cut through the churchyard and were on the track down to the river did she wonder why he was really there.

'Well, this is most agreeable,' he began. 'A far cry from the hot sands of Arabia.'

'Do you spend a lot of time there?' All she knew of Vaughn was that he was SIS's Deputy Director for the Middle East.

'At least half of it. The rest is in London. I shouldn't complain, of course. You don't get to pick or choose in the Service, do you?'

'No.'

They walked on. He helped her over a stile, and they were into a field, the dogs rootling around in the nearest hedge.

'Enjoying your week in the country? From what

I hear about your last mission, you deserve a bit of relaxation.'

Relaxation? There were the nightmares that left her cowering in a corner, shivering, bathed in sweat. There were the times when the ordinary world was like a creaky old stage play, in which everyone was speaking tired lines in front of wobbling scenery, and she was the only one who could see the farce for what it was.

And there was Peter.

'Only we may need your help.'

They walked on, until he took her silence as agreement that he could lay out his stall.

'Have you heard of a place called Ahmar? The Emirate of Ahmar?' She shook her head. 'No reason why you should. It's in the Gulf. Not much more than a town and a lot of scrubby desert with a few camels. Most of their revenue comes from trade across the Persian Gulf. Or rather, it did. That part of the desert turns out to float on a sea of oil and suddenly Ahmar is what our American cousins call an *asset*.

'We provide the Emir with a mix of guidance and protection, while he gets on with ruling his people. Like Oman, or the Trucial States. It's worked pretty well down the years. But to be honest, it helped that no-one else was very interested. Now we have the Soviets, the Americans, even the Persians and the Iraqis flexing their muscles.

'The Emir, Rashid, is in failing health. In June, he's holding a *Shura* – that's a kind of tribal Parliament – to confirm his chosen successor. It's not automatically the eldest son. Instead, the Emir chooses a Crown Prince from amongst his sons, brothers and so on. This can lead to a lot of tension over the succession. Rashid has three sons – legitimate ones, that is – and there are plots and factions galore.

'The Emir is about to start a course of radiotherapy at the American Hospital in Beirut. His plan is to fly up there each week, have the treatment session, and then fly back the next day. We think someone might use this chance to get him out of the way, before the *Shura*.'

'How?'

'One possibility is a bomb. But whoever were to succeed in succeeding' – Vaughn allowed himself a little smile at his own witticism – 'would be tainted by the assumption that he was the one who had arranged Rashid's murder. Not a great start for the new regime.'

'Would that matter?' Clemency tried to match Vaughn's cynical tone. 'Maybe he'd want to be seen as a ruthless ruler.'

'A fair point. But he might come across as just a little bit too ruthless. For reasons I'll come on to in a moment, Rashid will be travelling back and forth using a commercial airliner on a scheduled service. If he goes up in smoke, so do another fifty passengers and crew.'

'Oh.'

'Quite. That's why our aviation security people think that a hijacking is more likely. They could put the plane down on an abandoned airstrip somewhere in the desert, take the Emir away, and then leave the plane and the other passengers to be rescued once the rest of the world woke up to what was going on. Of course, the Emir would never be seen alive again.'

'But if you know about the plot, can't you – or the Emir, or whoever – can't you just hire a private plane? Or fly the doctors down to his palace?'

'We've tried, believe me. The problem is, he's a stubborn old man with a lot of pride. He's happy to take advice from the Resident Advisor, and from his

Vizier – that's a kind of prime minister. But once he's made his mind up, it's incredibly difficult to shift him.'

There were a couple of fishermen by the mill-pool, so he fell silent, leaving Clemency to wonder where she could possibly fit into this tangled tale. She'd never been to the Middle East and didn't speak a word of Arabic. She knew nothing of the country, the people or the politics. She knew even less about oil, airlines, or the task of stopping leaders from being assassinated. But some small detail must have led someone at SIS to think – *ah, that's a job for a woman*. Protecting the Emir's wife, perhaps? More likely a daughter at school or even at university in England.

By the time they had left the fishermen behind and Vaughn was ready to resume his story, Clemency had prepared her excuses. She had volunteered for espionage, to take Peter's place until he was released by the KGB, but she wasn't sure she wanted to be turned into a bodyguard or a babysitter.

'I can't see how this is anything to do with me. Wouldn't it be better to—'

'If you'd indulge me a little longer?' Vaughn cut in. 'As you so rightly pointed out, the simple answer would be for him to hire a private plane. But the Emir happens to have a substantial share in an airline of his own. It's a source of immense pride to him. He won't countenance admitting that he's scared to use it.

'This means we have to work on the assumption that the Emir will be flying to and from the Lebanon every week for six weeks, and that during that time, there will be an attempt to hijack the plane, or possibly to destroy it with a bomb. This is absolutely not in Britain's interest. Ahmar is in a highly strategic location on the Persian Gulf. A quarter of the world's oil shipments pass offshore. It has an excellent natural harbour of the kind that the Soviet Navy would love to have in the region.'

She looked at him sharply. 'The Soviets?'

'Oh yes. This is about more than which of the Emir's sons fights his way to the throne. Moscow might provoke a civil war, just like in the Yemen. There are rumours that Mohammed, one of Rashid's sons, is close to the Soviet consul. They might use their influence, maybe even their money, to ensure his succession, in return for kicking us out and letting them in.

'That brings me to you. Yesterday we convened a sub-committee to look at the security aspects of the situation. We've reviewed procedures on the ground and in the air, and how to identify any suspect activity. To avoid showing our hand, we have to use people who would be on the plane anyway. People who would have a reason for walking up and down, checking on the passengers.'

'The crew.'

'Spot on. Now you might say, take one of our people and put them on board as a steward. But one of the... er... selling points of this airline, which rejoices in the name of Red Air, is that it only has stewardesses. And that is the very long story that leads up to you and I walking along this charming river-bank.'

'You want me to pretend to be a stewardess? I couldn't do that.'

'We'd provide some training, of course. The boss of the airline is an old friend of ours. In any case, what we are looking for is a bit of flexibility and initiative, and Swan assures me that you have that in spades.'

'That's very nice of him,' she said dryly.

'He also said that you had a particular commitment to

the cause. That if there were the chance to do some work that truly mattered, then you'd be keen to take it on.'

There was a question-mark floating over his words, as if she were in some way letting the side down. After Argentina, she'd sworn never to take an operation at face value again. But the last thing in the world she wanted was to be dropped by the Service. She had promised herself – promised Peter, though he didn't know it – that she would see this though until he returned.

'I'm sorry. I suppose it's the responsibility. How on earth am I supposed to spot if someone is carrying a gun? They'll be professionals. They won't be fidgeting and checking their watches and giving themselves away.'

'You leave the responsibility to us,' Vaughn said smoothly. 'We think you're the right one for this, and you can only do your best.'

She began to dig at the ground with the toe of her boot. A voice at the back of her mind was telling her to say no – or more like, screaming it at her. Deep down, she was scared. She saw a peaceful flight being turned in a flash into a nightmare, the plane breaking apart in mid-air, spilling its passengers across the sky.

All her life, she'd thought she had courage. Was this what cowardice was like?

Meanwhile Vaughn was talking, his voice casual, natural, but his eyes studying her intently.

'There's one other thing, if this helps you to make up your mind. We know who is heading up the GRU operation in the region.'

Even before he spoke, she knew what he was going to say; who that man was.

Petrov.

It made her more frightened than ever.

'When do I leave?'

# 2

There were five men in the conference room at Farnborough. One was stuffing tobacco into his pipe, another intently studying a file; two – one in RAF blue – were chatting like old friends, and at the far end of the table, a scientist type with patches on his tweed jacket was seated in a world of his own, completing *The Times* crossword. No-one paid any attention as she entered. They would think she was a secretary or messenger.

'You must be the mysterious Miss White.'

She hadn't noticed the man beside the door. He was tall, dark-haired, in his late twenties and with a friendly grin. He held out his hand.

'My name is Fletcher. David Fletcher. I'm your oppo from Five.'

She looked completely blank.

'Your opposite number. From the Security Service. We'll be working together in Ahmar.'

'I'm sorry, but I really don't know anything about any of this yet. I only heard about it on Friday afternoon.'

'Really? Well, as I understand it, I'm going to be riding shotgun in the plane whenever the Emir's on board, and you're going to be helping out by keeping an eye on the passengers.'

'Do you mean shotgun as in with a gun?'

'It shouldn't come to that. Ah, we begin.'

Vaughn arrived, and there was a move to sit down. She took the seat next to David, assuming they would start at once, but Vaughn and the man who'd been reading the file were now talking in low voices in the far corner. Secrets within secrets.

'I take it you're new to all this,' David said quietly. 'Or you'd realise the historic dimension to this meeting.'

'I am,' she replied. 'What am I missing?'

'The thing is, your mob and mine tend to have as little to do with each other as possible. You think we're all flatfooted coppers with no finesse, and we think you're all pederasts. Obviously, that doesn't apply in your case. But the fact remains that the whole world is split into two – Britain, the Commonwealth and the Empire is for MI5, and the rest for MI6, and woe betide anyone who crosses those boundaries. This is different. For once, we have to work together.'

'Why?'

'Because Ahmar reports to the Political Resident, Persian Gulf in Bahrain, who oversees the Trucial States. As they're a kind of outpost of Empire, it counts as MI5 territory. But Beirut is in the Lebanon, which belongs to MI6. As the Emir's plane will be shuttling back and forth between the two, we have to co-operate, straight down the line, including having a representative from each Service on board.'

'How ridiculous.'

'Isn't it? The sensible thing would have been for one of our young ladies to work with me. But that would have meant loss of face for MI6.'

'Are you all right with that?'

'Miss White, I just want to get home in one piece. In a spirit of self-preservation, I hope we can form an effective team.'

'Gentlemen... Miss...'

They were called to order by the man with the file, who introduced himself as John Farringdon, head of the Persian Gulf desk at the Security Service.

'So, this is the second meeting of the Blue Dove committee. I won't waste time on going through it all again. As you remember, last week we decided to ask the Air Ministry for a technical appraisal of the threat. Wing Commander Ward of the Air Accident Investigation Branch here at Farnborough specialises in airline sabotage. How many incidents have you investigated personally, did you say?'

'Six. Of course, there's lots of theoretical work too.'

'I believe you have a plane for us to look over?'

'That's right,' the Wing Commander said with a gleam of enthusiasm. 'But first, it might help if I explain the basic principles of destroying an aircraft through sabotage.'

He stood up and lifted the cloth away from a blackboard set up in one corner. Tacked to it was a poster showing a passenger plane in cut-away, revealing every panel and wire in loving detail.

'There are essentially four ways to bring down an airliner in flight. The first,' Ward tapped the cockpit with his pointer, 'is to incapacitate the crew. If no-one knows how to fly the plane, it will crash. You might just be able to talk someone down from the control tower, but unfortunately that depends on them knowing how to use the plane's radio.'

'The second is fire. Planes are very vulnerable to that. They're full of flammable materials, from aviation spirit to foam seats. A fire, particularly in the baggage hold here, would be very likely to bring down a plane.

You'd have the advantage that it would probably be considered accidental.'

'This could be a critical point, and we'll come back to this later,' Farringdon said. 'Sorry, do go on.'

'Baggage and cargo are the most likely, but all that can be searched, so long as you know what to look for. On some planes, including the Viscount, you can access the baggage hold in flight. I wouldn't fancy trying it myself, but you could get down there with a smoke mask and a fire extinguisher. So a better place would be somewhere entirely out of sight, such as in the insulation between the cabin interior and the outer skin of the plane. Then you'd be able to get a real blaze going before anyone realised.'

'Little ray of sunshine, isn't he?' David whispered.

'The third vulnerability is fuel. Deliberate contamination can lead to an aircraft's engines failing, and in theory you could also put too little fuel in the plane and rig up the gauges to hide this. Either way, if the plane were over the sea, or over mountainous terrain, then you'd have a crash. The flip side of that, though, is that even if all the engines fail, a plane can still glide a surprising distance. That would give the crew the chance to put down safely. That's perfectly feasible if you're flying over the desert.

'But the most direct – certainly the most popular – approach is a bomb. Even a small device can cause a catastrophic decompression.'

'Where would you put it, Wing Commander?' Farringdon was feeding him with questions like the straight man to a stage comedian.

'That depends on what kind of access you have to the aircraft. If it were left unguarded, then my own preference would be to put it in the empennage

– what's commonly called the tail – just beyond the end of the pressure bulkhead here. That's a particularly vulnerable spot.'

'What size of bomb are we talking about?'

'In the right place, you might only need a few pounds of plastic explosive and a detonator.'

'And there'd be a timer? Does this mean we could vary the times of the flights to try and reduce the risk?'

'By all means, but I'm inclined to think it won't be a timer as such. After all, we all know that airliners don't always stick to schedule, and if the bomb went off on the ground it wouldn't do much damage. That's why an altimeter trigger would be ideal, set to detonate while the plane is climbing to its cruising altitude of, say, 35,000 feet.'

'What would happen to the plane if the bomb went off at that height?' Clemency asked. Beneath his bristling moustache, the Wing Commander suppressed a smile.

'It would crash.'

'I understand that,' Clemency said once the laughter around the table had subsided. 'What I mean is, would the plane fall to pieces? Or would there be any chance of landing it safely?'

'Ah, yes, fair point. That's why the tail is the most vulnerable point. The loss of the weight of the tail would pitch the nose down sharply and the plane would enter a near-vertical dive. There would be no prospect of pulling out without the tail plane, and indeed without the rudder the aircraft would probably enter a severe spin around the lateral axis.'

'How long would it take to reach the ground?'

'From 35,000 feet? Well...' the Wing Commander was quite pleased with this challenge. 'Say pitched at five degrees to the vertical, and attaining say Mach 0.85…' He absented himself in mathematics for a few moments. 'Probably just less than two minutes.'

They paused for a moment to contemplate what those two minutes would be like for those on board.

'Presumably they wouldn't know much about it,' Vaughn said.

'I'm afraid it's not that simple,' Ward replied. 'The passengers might be rendered unconscious by anoxia, but the pilots have full oxygen masks by their seats. The flight attendants have portable oxygen bottles and masks, the idea being they can then help any passengers who are struggling to breathe.'

Farringdon leaned forward impatiently.

'Let's get back to thinking about how to avoid this happening in the first place. If I may sum up, the Emir's aeroplane could be brought down in flight by a bomb the size of a shoebox, if it's planted in the right place. The making of the bomb is straightforward. And if that weren't enough, there have been several cases of planes blown up in just this way that anyone could read about in the papers.'

The others exchanged looks, but there was nothing there to disagree about.

'To prevent this, we need to have a constant guard on the plane in the Lebanon and in Ahmar.'

'And in any other airport where the plane flies to,' the Wing Commander added cheerfully. 'Remember, you could combine a seven-day timer with an altimeter, and so you could plant the bomb days in advance, and it would only go off at a particular time and when the plane was in the air.'

Farringdon was starting to look harried.

'Right. We have to guard the plane day and night, at

a range of different locations.'

'The opposition will probably know those locations in advance.' This from the Air Ministry man.

'Before we get into all that, shall we go and look at the plane?'

*

From the ground, the Viscount managed to look both elegant and substantial: ready to take gracefully to the air and strong enough to survive once it was there.

The Wing Commander was at Clemency's side.

'Lovely ship, isn't it?'

He sounded so enthusiastic, she wondered how much of his motivation for his work came from protecting the planes themselves, not the passengers inside.

'So,' he said more loudly, with the rest of the committee standing loosely around him. 'This is an example of the Vickers Viscount 700 series. You've probably all flown in them at one point or another, as BEA use them extensively on their European routes.

'Four engines, Rolls Royce Darts, quiet, very reliable. Range of up to 2,500 nautical miles. Seating for between forty and fifty passengers, depending on the configuration. Toilet is usually at the front, galley at the rear. Passengers enter through the rear door, crew through the front. You'll see it's quite low to the ground. You can reach up and get access to the wheel recesses and the hold quite easily. It doesn't need a special ladder or anything.'

They followed him up a set of metal stairs and into the cabin. There were four quite comfortable-looking seats in each row, with a narrow aisle in between, and the unusually large windows made it feel spacious.

'If you look here, where they've taken the interior panels down, you can see the skin of the aircraft. This is about three-eights of an inch thick. You could cut it with a pair of garden shears. That's why if there's a break in the skin, from a bomb, then it can rip quite easily. Now come and look at this...'

Clemency gazed down the length of the cabin. With the rows of seats, it had something of the feel of a very long and thin theatre – one where she would soon, apparently, be playing the part of a stewardess. It all felt a little unreal, even more so when Ward called them to the galley at the back of the plane, a cramped space lined with steel cabinets and racks of flat ovens for warming the food. Ward explained in some detail the consequences of a breach of the rear bulkhead – the decompression, the potential loss of the whole tail structure, the likelihood that anything in the area would be sucked into the void.

David appeared at her side.

'Well done for asking about what would happen if we fluff this.'

'I felt such a fool,' she replied.

'You were quite right to ask. I've nothing against any of these chaps, but they won't be there, will they?'

'How did you get dragged into this?'

'All my own fault. A few months ago, they asked for a volunteer for a course the FBI were running on aircraft security. I thought a month in the States would be just the ticket. Little did I realise I'd end up spending six weeks on a flying bomb.'

'Don't say that.'

'I imagine Ahmar will be a complete armpit. I've been to a couple of other Gulf states and the climate is lousy and the living conditions truly awful. At least you'll be in Beirut.'

'Will I?'

'That's where the Red Air crews are based. Cafés, bars... The Paris of the East, they call it.'

'What did they teach you on the course?'

'The signs to look for in a terrorist or hijacker. Most of it's pretty basic, to be honest. They have a lot of planes being hijacked to Cuba and apparently you have people turning up for a flight to Canada in midwinter wearing short-sleeved shirts and no coats. They know they're actually going to the Caribbean. Or they ask all sorts of questions about where they're sitting or exactly what route the plane will be taking.

'We also had a lot of time on a firing range they've got set up like the inside of an airliner cabin. They have these special bullets that won't do too much damage to the aircraft if you miss the hijackers. Luckily we've never needed that kind of thing over here.'

He spoke as if it were all a bit of a game. But firing bullets into cardboard targets wasn't the same as hitting flesh and bone. She studied him as he gazed at the plane, with all the enthusiasm of a boy with a new toy, and wondered how he would be when reality broke in.

*

Once the meeting was over, the Wing Commander offered Clemency a lift back to the station. First they went to pick up some papers from his office. This was part of a huge brick and corrugated-iron hangar, but at the door he stopped, oddly embarrassed.

'Would you prefer to wait outside, Miss White?'

'I don't mind,' she replied. 'Is it top top secret?'

'Er, no. I'm afraid it's another Viscount. It's not a pretty sight. It was the one that crashed outside Dusseldorf back in March, if you recall.'

She did. It had been all over the papers – a modern airliner flying in good weather suddenly falling out of the sky. None of the passengers or crew had survived. From what she could remember of the pictures of the crash site, not much would have remained of the bodies.

'We're reconstructing the wreckage on a frame. Standard procedure.'

She followed him into the hangar where, under dozens of harsh fluorescent strip lights, there stood a cloud of fragments of twisted and burned metal, some no bigger than a tea-towel, held in place by hundreds of thin steel rods and making the outline of the aircraft. It was like a work of avant-garde art, a modernist sculpture, the kind of thing that sent the older art critics into a fury.

'We're almost done with positioning,' Ward said, more at ease now he could return to lecturing. 'We recovered over eighty percent of the craft, so it's been fairly straightforward. Not like the Comets. They fell over the sea, if you recall. We're particularly interested in the rear cargo door and the controls of course. Come and see.'

He led her to the rear of the assembly. Up close, she could see the black stains of burning and the blistered paint on the metal of the fuselage and feel the force that had been unleashed when the plane hit the ground. When she looked inside the cabin, there were the seats, scorched and blackened, bent over, twisted together, and she thought of the people who had been strapped into them.

'These bundles of wires,' she asked at random. 'Do they go to the cockpit?'

She didn't care; but pride made her want to say something.

'That's right. Usually, they'd be out of sight under the floor. They're in tension, so in the crash they tend to curl up like that. The heat too, of course.'

The cabin was lit by the hundred of tears in the outer skin of the plane. At the far end was the cockpit, where the pilots would have fought in vain to save the plane. Two minutes to reach the ground, Ward had said.

Almost next to her was what was left of the galley. Was that where the stewardesses had been, strapped into their jump seats for the final moments before the end? Or had the disintegration of the tail sent them tumbling into the void?

It was black, a funeral pyre. Faint, but pervasive, came the smell of a bonfire put out with water before its time, acrid and cloying; and behind that, something else – the tang of bleach. The whole of the inside must have been covered in human remains, and they would have had to disinfect it – as if the entire reconstruction was a kind of morgue.

It was horrible to look at, this ghost of the plane – unreal and frightening.

'Seen enough?' Ward asked.

She nodded, not trusting herself to speak.

# 3

Vaughn had put together a briefing programme for David and Clemency, almost all about the politics of Ahmar and the neighbouring states. This was useful for David, who'd be staying in Ahmar except for the trips to Beirut with the Emir. But Clemency was both bored and fed up to be trailing around Whitehall in his wake. The worst was with Philip Martin in the Foreign Office, who delivered a lecture on the politics of the region without once looking at her.

'I think the best parallel is Saudi Arabia,' he said in his cold, precise voice. 'King Saud and his brother Prince Faisal have been locked in a power struggle for two years. Saud went abroad for medical treatment and Faisal formed a new government in his absence. When he came back, Saud ordered his guards to surround Faisal's palace. That's how things are done.

'Anyway, Ahmar is facing some of the same turmoil, on a much smaller scale. The Emir has three sons. Abdullah is the eldest. He's our man, in that he's not as bad as the others and believes in strong ties to the West. The only drawback is he's lazy and much too fond of the gambling tables of the South of France.

'Mohammed is the middle son, and he's the one we're pretty sure is planning this coup. He studied law in Paris after the war and picked up some radical ideas. He's a sharp operator and he could be working with Nasser without our knowing. It's perfectly respectable in Arab circles – even these conservative kingdoms – to have dealings with Egypt. Nasser might be a radical and a republican, but he still has a huge following amongst ordinary Arabs. Mohammed might privately promise all kinds of things in return for his help.

'But we can't entirely rule out Suleiman. He's the youngest by some way. He's close to the Salafists, the politically-active clerical movement. When we talked about someone giving their life to blow up the plane, it's the Salafists who might provide a volunteer. There would be clerics willing to declare it was a holy act against infidel invaders. Red Air spends its time taking its passengers to and from the bars, casinos and brothels of Beirut and Istanbul, with stewardesses who dress like *houris*, so it's a doubly-attractive target.'

He said this with icy relish, as if ridding the world of Red Air was a public service.

'Each brother has his own mini-court of hangers on and riff-raff, and naturally we have informants in each one. As I said, Mohammed is the real threat because of Nasser. Even Suleiman would be better. His rhetoric is anti-Western, but he's someone I expect we could do business with if we had to. After all, what form of Islam they follow is no concern of ours.'

'Are any family members travelling in the Emir's party?' David asked.

'Only his daughter-in-law, Fatima. She married Kader, who was the Emir's second son, but he was killed in a car crash about five years ago. They had one son, Khalid, who's at school in England. She trained as a doctor, in Paris, before she married, so at least he'll be in good hands on the plane. He'll also be accompanied by his secretary, a chap called Hamid, and by a couple of men from the Royal bodyguard, no doubt armed to the teeth like bandits from a comic opera.'

'What about the Soviets?' Clemency asked. 'Which brother would they back?'

'It's more complex than that,' Martin replied, looking at David. 'The Soviets tend to work through their client states in the region – Egypt, Syria and so on. They provide technical support, but try and remain behind the scenes. I suppose you couldn't rule out Moscow sending one or two of their people to help pull a conspiracy together...'

He said it as if it was an irrelevance; but to Clemency, it was the crux. If Moscow sent Petrov, and the conspiracy was broken, he might fall into their hands. Who better to be exchanged for Peter than the man who had captured him in the first place?

Over lunch in the Foreign Office canteen, she asked David about the Soviet involvement; but he was surprisingly dismissive.

You're seeing Reds under the Bedouins,' he joked. 'Me, I always go for the simplest explanation. In this case, that's family rivalries. In any case, our chaps in Ahmar would know if the Soviets were active.'

'Your 'chaps' don't even seem to know which brother is behind this plot.'

'Put your claws away, Clemency,' he said with a disarming smile. 'I'm on your side, remember? Anyway, the most likely reason for that is that there's nothing behind these rumours in the first place. You and I are going to have a six-week holiday at the tax-payer's expense, that's all. You can top up your tan, buy a fake Persian rug and be home for Christmas.'

*

Clemency had three days before she was due in Beirut. She couldn't face the thought of going home again, or even seeing her friends in London. She had to look ahead to the mission, not to what remained of her old life. She was already booked on a flight back anyway. And in Bern was the only one who would understand what she was going through, and why.

Lucinda Jensen was an old colleague of Peter's from the wartime Special Operations Executive, now working as the confidential secretary to the chief of one of the city's largest commercial banks. At Peter's request, she had shared with Clemency some of the skills an agent needed to survive, from shaking of a tail to the basics of martial arts. Without this knowledge, Clemency might already be dead.

Most of all, the two of them shared Peter. He had obviously been close to Lucinda back in SOE, though Clemency had been careful not to find out how close. Lucinda still cared for him, and in the months since Peter's capture, Clemency had passed on every scrap of information that Swan and his colleagues at SIS had let slip. In return, Lucinda had been her confessor and her nurse, helping to put her back together after the debacle of Argentina.

At the post office, she lingered over her telegram form. She had to make her meaning clear to Lucinda and hide it from anyone else, all at nine pence a word. In the end she wrote:

JENSEN OSTALPENBANK BERN PERSONAL RETURNING TOMORROW MUST MEET MUCH GOSSIP STOP ALSO OFFERED SHARES REDAIR STOP QUERY GOOD INVESTMENT OR POLITICAL RISKS AHMAR TOO GREAT LOVE CLEMENCY

Lucinda would understand. She'd often spoken of how, across the globe, the secretaries and personal assistants to the great men of industry and commerce formed a discreet network of their own. Lucinda would soon have information that would never reach the ears of Vaughn and the others. Most of all, it would be gathered to help Clemency and Peter, not filtered to suit the hidden motives of SIS or MI5.

She walked back to the Foreign Office along the edge of St James's Park. It was a beautiful afternoon, very still, the leaves poised to fall in the next breath of air, little sound except for the distant drone of traffic and the occasional cackle of a duck on the lake; the chill in the air conjuring up crumpets and open fires.

It would be scenes like this that would be keeping Peter sane, whether in Moscow or Siberia. There would be torture, and neglect, and drugs and sleep deprivation; but he could always close his eyes and be back in England; and he would have the belief – the absolute belief – that he would never be forgotten; that somewhere, there were people who cared and who were working to bring him home.

She blinked away her tears.

Swan and the others: they'd told her they'd get him back. Maybe she was like Peter – she had to trust them, or she'd go mad. And they'd talked about their successes, agent swaps and so on. A man called Janner. And another – she forgot his name now – a MI6 officer kidnapped by the Gestapo in 1939. No-one had heard from him for the length of the war. Then, when it was over, and they opened up the concentration camps, there he was.

'Apparently he was no different than the day they caught him,' Swan had said with a rare chuckle. 'As if those six years never happened. Went home to his wife in Pinner and his roses. I'm told he was even more arrogant than his German captors, and that got him through.'

So Peter would come home; and Clemency would be there for him.

# 4

It was a bleak morning, grey and with a chill wind coming straight down from the Alps, and the bears were sulking in their artificial caves. It was where Clemency and Peter had come when he first asked for her help on one of his missions. The café was deserted, and their coffee was cold even before it reached their lips. As she passed on to Lucinda the little she had learned about Peter, their spirits were equally depressed.

'It wouldn't have been like this in the war.' Lucinda's voice, usually so smooth, had an edge of anger. 'If there was any chance of getting one of our people back, we took it. Bribes, blackmail, arranging a prison breakout. It might not have made sense, just for one man, but you still did it.'

'They say they have no-one to exchange.'

Lucinda waved this away impatiently.

'It's sheer stupidity. How do we keep our own people on-side, if they think they might be left in the lurch like this? It's hard enough to take the risks without fearing you're seen as expendable.'

They lapsed into silence. A crow landed on the terrace, scattering the other birds, and began to peck awkwardly at a discarded crust.

'How do you feel about going up against Comrade Petrov?'

'I don't know. Scared? Terrified? I've seen him kill people in cold blood. He didn't care any more than if he were snuffing out a candle.'

She looked away, seeing Petrov's men bundling the bodies into the car, scuffing the pools of blood on the dusty road.

'No-one would think any less of you if you sat this one out. If he sees you, he'll recognise you. That puts you in danger.'

'I know. But I can't... I can't just leave it to someone else.'

'I'm so very grateful to you, Clemency,' Lucinda said gently. 'You really are Peter's last hope. I only wish I could do more to help.'

Clemency blushed. Lucinda was old enough – just – to be her mother. She was also, in some way, a rival for Peter's affections. She admired Lucinda, was a little afraid of her, and jealous too, and this mix made it hard for her to accept her praise.

'Anyway,' Luicinda said, sitting back, suddenly brisk. 'Shall I tell you what I've learned about Red Air? You might not like it.'

'Is it dangerous?' Clemency's mind had kept going back to the wreckage of the plane at Farnborough, and she had hated every minute of the flight out to Bern.

'Oh no, nothing like that. I just wondered if London explained what you were getting in to, pretending to be a stewardess with Red Air. You see, it's what they call a nightclub line. All glamour and razzmatazz. Cocktails as you get on board and pop music playing. It's an American thing, I'm told. They use the stewardesses to sell the flights. It's all *Come Fly With Me* – as if they spend their time being chatted up by Frank Sinatra or Dean Martin.'

'If only.'

'I remember seeing one of their planes in Nicosia.

The whole thing was painted bright red, with a kind of devils' face on the tail. When they started, they had the stewardesses dressed as devils, but that didn't last long. You could tell that a man thought of that one. Of course, the passengers used to pull their tails.'

Clemency smiled along, but she wondered if she were the only one at the meeting in Farnborough who hadn't realised that Red Air was a bit of a joke.

'Alec Rossiter is the man who runs it. He was with Transport Command in the war and then, like a hundred other pilots, he left the RAF and started a charter airline with a couple of war-surplus Dakotas. British Falcon. Unlike most of the others, he had a head for business and was still around in '47 for the Berlin Airlift. He did well out of the Korean War, then moved into package tours. But what he really wanted was a scheduled airline, with scheduled profits – a bit like Thompson is doing at Caledonian, or Laker with British United. That's where Red Air comes in.'

She broke off to signal to the waiter, standing disconsolate in the shelter of the café's awning, to bring them more coffee.

'Where was I? Oh yes, so there were several airlines that had set up after the war in the Gulf, mainly to service the oil industry. Flying in equipment, men, and so on. But Rossiter had a different angle. He saw that, sooner or later, all this oil would start to make the Gulf states rich. And there was nothing to spend your money on, so it would create a new class of well-off Arabs who'd want to travel.

'Beirut was the natural base. Have you been there? It has all the beaches, casinos and nightclubs that an Arab millionaire could ever want. But the Lebanon already has Middle East Airlines. So his idea was to register his airline in one of the smaller Gulf states, and use it to build a network that would service the whole region. The airline would be run from Beirut, but would act like the national airline of the host state.

'That's the plan he hawked around the Gulf states in '59, and the Emir of Ahmar, whom I'm told by an American chum is a very shrewd cookie, agreed for the new airline to be based there, so long as he could take a major stake in it. That suited Rossiter, because the Emir's money meant he could get started on a much larger scale. That's how Red Air was born.'

Clemency was amazed by how Lucinda had amassed this information in such a short time, just sitting at her desk in the bank. It was far more helpful than anything Vaughn had provided. It must be so frustrating for her, to have such a grip on finance and international business and yet be excluded from it, to be the secretary, not the boss.

'Does Rossiter know about the threat to the Emir?' Lucinda asked.

'He has to. There's no way we could be on board without his say-so.'

'Can he be trusted?'

'I'm meeting him in Beirut. He said he was very curious to see his newest stewardess.'

'Well, there's one other thing I was told about Rossiter by my Board of Trade contact. I was a bit cynical and said it sounded like Red Air matters more to him than anything else, including the best interests of his own country. She said I might be right, but not right enough. What matters most to Rossiter is Rossiter. There is nothing – nothing – that he wouldn't do to advance his interests.'

It took Clemency a while to follow this through;

and then she wanted to laugh.

'Are you saying he'd let the Emir be killed to get in with the new regime?'

She waited for Lucinda's denial. But it didn't come.

'But that would mean fifty people dead,' she protested. 'The loss of one of his own planes.'

Lucinda raised an elegant eyebrow, as if surprised at Clemency's naivety.

'I expect he's well-insured.'

# 5

Rome; Nicosia; now the BOAC Comet was approaching the coast of the Lebanon. Waves crashing against the rocks, sandy coves with fishing boats: it could have been Cornwall, except for the intensity of the light and the dusty fields that stretched away towards snow-capped mountains. Then they were passing apartment blocks and hotels, with the occasional minaret or spire, all in the same rose-pink as the rocks, so that they seemed to grow from the land itself. A marina, swimming pools, and then they were turning again, sky and land wheeling away, and all Clemency could see was the sea, disconcertingly close. Even once they were level again they appeared to be descending gently towards a water landing, until they slipped over the edge of the runway and touched down safely.

It was wonderfully warm, with everyone in shirt sleeves or cotton dresses. Even the immigration officer produced a big smile as he handed her back her passport and wished her a pleasant stay. The sense of being at the gateway to the East came from all sides; the exotic planes on the apron – Olympic, Middle East Airlines, Air India and Gulf Air; the equally exotic uniforms of the crews strolling through the arrivals halls; and then she was met by a woman in the most exotic of all, dressed head to toe in red.

'Miss Green? I'm Felicity Clarke, from Red Air.'

She was Clemency's age, her blonde hair sculpted into a chignon, made up in the latest London fashion with long eyelashes and liner; but something still suggested a background of horses and country walks.

'How was your flight out?' she asked, leading Clemency back through the arrivals hall. 'At least it was on a jet. When we have home leave we have to go with British Falcon and that means a DC6. It takes hours and you can't hear properly for a week.'

She had a much more relaxed manner than the BOAC stewardesses. At first Clemency thought this was because they were to be colleagues. But as she listened to Felicity's chatter about Beirut's many attractions and how much fun she'd have showing her round, she realised it was that on BOAC they had spoken as if acting the part of a debutante, mincing and refined. Felicity really was from that world, but she chose to speak with the flatter vowels of Chelsea and Soho.

She led Clemency through a set of doors marked ACCES INTERDIT and into a long corridor, up some stairs and into a large room with pigeon-holes along one wall, maps on another, windows looking out over the airport in front of them. The rest of it was taken up with armchairs and low tables. It was empty except for a man in shirt sleeves reading a paperback.

'Home from home. Or the crew room, if you prefer. Ops is through there, the lav is there, and changing rooms down the corridor, though the Boss likes us to be in uniform as much as possible. Free advertising. John, have you seen the Boss?'

The man didn't look up.

'He's in G-ARIF. He said to take the new girl out there.'

This meant more corridors and stairs until they emerged onto the tarmac. There were no locks or keys or checks on who was coming or going, and Clemency wondered how they planned to keep the planes safe overnight.

'This is Freddy.' Felicity pointed to a plane about fifty yards away. It was painted all over in bright scarlet, except for the airline name along the cabin and the devil on the tail. It was so garish it took Clemency a moment to realise it was the same kind of plane she'd seen at Farnborough.

They climbed up the metal steps.

'Got her, Fliss?'

The voice was loud, working-class London, and the man who emerged from the cabin fitted it. He was large but fit, friendly enough but hard-edged if he needed to be. He was a little like Sergeant Morris at the Embassy in Bern, but without the ingrained deference to rank or class. He waited until Felicity had gone, then gestured to her to sit in one of the cabin seats. He stayed standing himself.

'I thought it would be helpful to have a word or two before you joined the team. I'm afraid I can't offer you any refreshment.'

She wondered if he were laughing at her, with his talk of refreshment; but from the point of view of security, it couldn't be bettered. With the cabin door shut, no-one could possibly overhear.

'I had a long chat with your Mr Vaughn last week. He filled me in on the general situation, and on your role. I should start by telling you I don't believe there's anything behind this talk of a plot. I don't mean he's wrong to take it seriously. The last thing I want is a bomb on one of my planes. But I know this part of the world pretty well by now and it will turn out to be nothing more than rumours. Right?'

'But if there is anything to it, do you have any ideas who is responsible?'

'I know it isn't Mohammed. I'm not saying he's not capable of something like this, but he doesn't need to do it. The Emir will choose him anyway. Also, I don't think it matters so much to him. He's more international in outlook than either of his brothers. He lives in France a lot of the time, and he's always travelling. Beyond that, I can't say. I've met both of the others from time to time, but not well enough to know what they might do if their backs were against the wall. But as I said, I think you'll have a pleasant few weeks out here, and then the Emir will have finished his treatment and we can all relax.'

'I hope so too.'

'Now, you'll be the second stewardess on Zebra Peter. In case you're wondering, that's the last two letters of the registration: G-ARZP. The Captain is Bill Macquarie, who's a bit of a dinosaur but a damn good pilot. His first officer is Mike Stannard. He came to us from BEA and one of our rising stars. He'll be a captain in a year or so. Both very experienced, but whatever you do, don't be bothering them. Your senior stewardess is Farzana Rahini, but she's rostered to be on another crew two days a week, and then Felicity will be there instead. They'll be in charge, and you need to do exactly what they say. Right?'

'Of course.'

'It means you'll get the worst jobs. That's just how it is. Like cleaning the toilet if anyone has an accident. For some of our passengers, it's the first time they've encountered a flushing toilet and there's a tendency for things to get stuck in them. If that happens, you'll need to get it out again. There's only one toilet on the Viscount and we can't just say it's out of order on a four-hour flight with fifty passengers. Right?

'Same if someone doesn't get to the sick bag in time. Mopping up is your job. The Viscounts fly above the worst of the weather, but it can get a bit choppy down in the Gulf, especially in the afternoon.'

Rossiter was relishing the idea of taking her down a notch; perhaps hoping she would object, so he could report her lack of cooperation back to Vaughn. She guessed he liked to be in control of those around him, and was finding her uncertain status – half-employee, half-independent – troubling. But she didn't care. Not if there were a chance of capturing Petrov.

'You'll be staying in the Rookery. It's a house in the old town with rooms for most of our crews, kitchens and so on. You'll have to share a room.'

'I'm sure it will all be fine.'

'I hope so. We want our stewardesses to have a bit of class about them, but we don't want stuck-up princesses. It's a bloody hard job, right?'

Clemency said nothing.

'Well, Miss Rahini will fill you in on the details. You'll meet her and the rest of the crew tomorrow at the Sporting Club. I've told Macquarie that you're from Customs and Excise, and the others that you're the daughter of an old pal of mine who can't quite think what to do with you and has asked me to give you a trial. I thought that would explain any lack of experience or competence on your part.'

'What should I do when we're not flying to Ahmar? Will I fly the other routes?'

'It'd look bloody odd if you didn't. You'll have

a flight to Nicosia one day and to Basra the other. You'll be with the same crew. The less you move about, the easier it is to get away with this play-acting, right? We'll provide overnight accommodation and expenses if needed. But no salary. Sorry to disappoint, if you thought you could earn that on top of whatever Vaughn's lot pay you.'

His desire to annoy her was so transparent that it just washed over her; but she was curious to know why he was doing this. Perhaps he wanted to test out how level-headed she was. Perhaps he simply wasn't a very nice man.

'Now if you didn't know already, out here in the Middle East, stewardesses are a bit of a sex symbol. That's all to the good. Helps publicise the airline. It means the passengers will chat you up. Good. Flirt back. It also means they'll ask you out. The rule is, you say no. That's for your protection as much as mine. If there's any trouble, complaints from a passenger, and it turns out you've been seeing them off the plane, then you're for the high jump. I don't care what you do. I'm not the moral police. I know what young girls are like these days. But get caught, and you're dead meat. Is that clear?'

'Mr Rossiter, I'm here to do a job, not find a husband.'

She'd kept her voice calm, but he must have seen how angry she was. He seemed pleased.

'One last thing. I run a safe airline, and an honest airline. I don't like my staff to pilfer, or steal from the passengers, or try and sneak stuff through customs or cheat on duty. Equally, I don't like snoopers. That's why I want you to promise to stick to what you're here for. If you find out about anything that looks iffy, I don't want you running off to Macquarie, or the local police, or your Mr Vaughn. You come to me, right? I'll decide what needs to be done. Is that OK?'

'Of course.'

'Good. Sorry if I've been blunt, but I find that's better in the long run. We all know exactly where we stand. Right? Now, I'll get one of the boys to run you into town.'

He led her towards the door, talking as he went.

'I hope you're as good as Vaughn says you are, you and this Mr Fletcher. The Emir is a tough old buzzard, but I don't want anything happening to him. And I definitely don't want to lose Zebra Peter. They're in your hands.'

'We'll look after him.'

'Good. Though if you don't, you won't be around to take the blame, will you?'

# 6

The taxi came into Beirut along the corniche, with the sea to one side and modern hotels and apartment blocks to the other. Ornate Art Nouveau street-lamps stood between palm trees and the French influence was evident in everything from the cafés to the local currency Clemency had exchanged at the airport, issued by the Banque du Liban.

The Rookery was a tall, thin building in a side street hardly wide enough for the taxi. With its green-painted shutters and peeling plaster, and the tattered remains of election posters, she could have been back in one of Paris's less glamorous districts. Her room was on the top floor, with two beds, a wash-stand and a plain desk. One bed was covered with a spread woven with rich colours: cinnamon and peacock blue, celadon and vermilion. This would belong to her new roommate, Farzana.

She glanced at the photo in a frame by the bed, showing a glamorous young man in an unfamiliar military uniform, and the small pile of books beside it. But there were people in the corridor outside and to be caught snooping would be a bad start. Instead, she dumped her bags on the other bed and went to the window. The street below was empty, save for a dog scratching around by a drain, but there was the sound of humanity all around, coming from behind the shuttered windows, everything from the crash of pans in a kitchen to a clarinet, or perhaps its Eastern cousin, playing a melancholy tune. When she looked up, there were the jumbled roofs, and the deepening blue of the sky as night fell, and a glimpse of snow-capped mountains.

She just had enough time to shower and change before her rendezvous at the Hotel Phoenicia with SIS's head of station in Beirut. Sitting at the bar by the outside pool, it was hard to think of anywhere more conspicuous for a discreet meeting. Everyone was there to see and be seen, the women in Balenciaga and Dior, the men in the kind of casual style that spoke of great wealth or status. There were French voices, American voices, a party of Germans or Austrians at the next table, and in the far corner a group of vaguely familiar faces clustered around a man who might be Dirk Bogarde.

'Miss Green?'

She turned to see a man in his fifties, a little like an ageing schoolboy with his round face and his greying hair flopping down over one eye. He was dressed in a cream linen suit that screamed Englishman abroad. But his eyes were soft and his manner diffident and she couldn't believe he was the one she was waiting for.

'I'm Charles Denholm. I hope you were expecting me?

'Oh yes, of course.'

He took his seat.

'Red wine? I'll join you in that.'

Even before he looked up a waiter appeared and took his order.

'Like it?' he asked, gesturing to their surroundings.

'Rather grand for a stewardess.'

'Oh, don't worry about that. The secret here is to

hide in plain sight. My cover is that I'm a reporter for the *International Petroleum Bulletin*. It means I can ask anyone I like about anything I like, because everything in this region comes back to oil, one way or another. But everyone who matters here knows what I really do. It's easier that way. Have you been to the Lebanon before?'

'No.'

'They call it the Switzerland of the Middle East. It's a bit more fun than that, but also a bit more precarious, as far as the relationships between the different communities goes. You have Christians, Sunni Muslims, Shia Muslims and Druze, and also hundreds of thousands of Palestinian refugees in the south. Lots of tensions. As a result, the Lebanese intelligence people, the *Sûreté Général*, have to be rather active. They're very co-operative with us, but they do like to know what's going on. By the way, the story is that I was at school with your father, which is why I'm keeping a bit of an eye on you while you're out here, and we'll probably meet for a drink or dinner from time to time.

'As I said, it's better to be open about these things. If we started meeting in odd places or using dead-letter drops the Lebanese would be all over us. I'll give you a number you can call day and night if you need to, but I don't think you will. As I understand it, the operation is being run out of Ahmar anyway. I'm just here if you need me.'

He talked a bit about the *Sûreté* and what to do if they made contact.

'What about the Soviets?' she asked. 'Will they be watching you?'

'I doubt it,' Denholm said. 'The Lebanese don't let

them operate here very much. They say that business in Lebanon is the true religion, with religion taking the place of politics, which doesn't leave much room for Left and Right. I think that's a bit glib, myself, but it's true there's no active Communist movement of any size. Shall we go and get something to eat?'

He had a car and a driver waiting outside and they set off at speed through the frantic Beirut traffic.

'Lots of cities claim to have the worst traffic in the world. Rome, Cairo, Bombay. I don't know how Beirut compares to those but I would say that crossing the street here is probably going to be the most dangerous thing you'll do while you're out here.'

'I hope so.'

The restaurant was in a back street, little more than an alley, and the entrance was just a plain doorway in an ancient stone wall. But inside the scent of the food was intoxicating, and the plain whitewashed walls and the dark-stained wooden floors and rafters were the ideal accompaniment to the succession of dishes that Denholm ordered in consultation with the host. He took such obvious pleasure in introducing her to it all, the flavoured rice, the lamb roasted in herbs, the ragout of grilled aubergines, that it really was like a family friend taking her under his wing.

'The problem with this kind of thing,' Denholm pronounced, spooning more *fattoush* onto her plate, 'is it makes it very difficult to think of returning to steak and kidney pudding and boiled cabbage.'

'How long have you been out here?'

'Since '43. I suppose I shouldn't complain when they say in London I've gone native. There are worse things to be than Lebanese. What do you make of Beirut, Miss Green?'

'I've only just arrived. How could I have anything worthwhile to say?'

'I've been here for over twenty years, but I can't pretend I understand the place. Not really. So my question is a genuine one. What do you think?'

Clemency had been told so much in the last week – by Vaughn, by the experts at Farnborough, and then by Rossiter – that it was refreshing to be asked her opinion about anything.

'It doesn't feel real to me, yet. The place does, the food and all this,' she said, taking in the low-ceilinged room, the other diners – they all seemed to be Lebanese, much more modestly dressed than at the Pheonecia, more like the doctors and lawyers and their wives from her parents' world. 'I mean the mission, I suppose. The whole thing sounds like a fairy tale. Or the Arabian Nights. *"There was a King and he had three sons..."* If it were real, you'd know who was plotting against him, even if you couldn't prove it. I know this is the East and everything's different here, but we're talking about someone capable of killing fifty innocent people. That's not normal. And for all three brothers to be capable of it? I just can't see it. So most of all, I find it hard to believe in it.'

'I see.' And he did seem to see, his eyes filled with concern. 'That's not good. I can't tell you much about Ahmar. I've never been there, and the Gulf is very different to the Levant. But even here there are political and dynastic troubles. Take Jordan. King Abdullah was assassinated in '51, and his son Tarif was forced out in '52. And Hussain, his grandson, is said to have a plane and a pilot permanently on stand-by to get him out if there's a coup. But I'm not trying to persuade you. If you're not convinced, you may have seen something, or sensed something, that the others haven't. There's nothing worse on an operation than everyone thinking the same way.'

'It won't stop me doing my job,' she reassured him. 'I understand you can't have every order you give being questioned. You must have some discipline. Some trust in the generals.'

It comforted her to repeat these words of Peter's, as if she were keeping the faith. But Denholm didn't look convinced.

'What exactly will you be doing?'

'Watching the passengers. Seeing if any of them look nervous or are carrying anything suspicious.'

'And then?'

'There's a man from MI5 on board. I'd let him know.'

Denholm looked quite pained.

'What does he do? Pull a gun on them? It all sounds like something from the Wild West.'

'If I do my job properly, we'll spot any trouble before we even take off. Anyway, I'm meeting the crew tomorrow. The Captain is called Macquarie.'

'The Australian? He's supposed to be a good thing. That might make a difference.'

Denholm fell into a reverie and Clemency concentrated on taking as much food as possible without looking greedy. Then the waiter returned with a fresh basket of flat bread and Denholm woke up.

'I hope you don't mind my saying this, Miss Green, but you're not quite what I expected.'

'I could say the same.' The excellent wine had loosened her tongue.

'There are very few women working in our world, and none of them are like you. I don't mean the tarts they hire in for honey traps. I mean officers. It wasn't always that way. During the war, some of the best agents – courage, intelligence – they were women. But not since then.'

She couldn't think what he was getting at, and silence seemed the best response.

'So I've begun to wonder why you're here.'

'I've been seconded from the Foreign Office. The rest of the time, I'm a cypher clerk.'

'That's all very well,' he said in his charming, diffident way. 'But that's just horseshit.'

She choked on a piece of lamb.

'It's a strange thing,' he went on, 'but the most dangerous thing in our world is suspicion. When you're on an operation, you have to believe in it. You have to think that London, or Beirut, or whoever – that they know what they're doing. That what you're risking your neck for is worth it. That they trust you. If you start picking away at that, it all falls apart. You see?'

'And you don't think I trust you?'

'You remember the Cambridge spies? Kim Philby lived here, you know, in Beirut. He'd left the Service under a cloud, but we still kept up with him. He was always good for keeping his ear to the ground. And good company. Then Nick Elliott came out to interview him, and before you know it, Kim was spirited away on a Soviet freighter and was next seen in Moscow. There were a lot of questions about who tipped him off and did he have friends protecting him, and as the Station chief I was on the receiving end of a lot of it. Paranoia creeps in. You start wondering what they make of your telegrams, or are they getting the Agency to check up on one. Every instruction you get, you think – is this a test? Or a trap? It's pure poison. Like a love affair going wrong. That's why I wonder, why are you here.'

'It's true about being a cypher clerk. I was lent to the station head, who was working under diplomatic cover at the Embassy in Bern. We… well, we became very close. And then he was snatched by the Soviets. I… I wanted to do something in return. He'd said it was like a war that no-one back home knew we were fighting. And in a war, you volunteer.'

'Peter Aspinall.' It was a statement, not a question.

'You know him?'

'Only by reputation. I'm sorry. It's a hell of a business. I'm sure… well, I hope they're doing everything to get him out.'

He made an effort to change the subject, asking about London, the latest films. When the meal was finished he was intrigued to find she knew and liked the Eastern style of thick sweet coffee. She explained that she had picked up a taste for it in Romania, and it clearly reassured him that she was experienced enough to have worked behind the Iron Curtain. But still he was solicitous as he dropped her back at the Rookery.

'As I said, Miss Green, do call me if you need anything, or if anything is worrying you. I don't mind false alarms.'

'I will.'

'Beirut is a safe place,' he said. 'A place you can relax and enjoy yourself. But what you're doing here isn't safe. Please don't ever forget that.'

She watched the taillights of his car disappear; and even then she waited, enjoying the warmth of the night, the scent from the jacaranda trees; but also watching to see if a car followed his, or if anyone were watching her.

Nothing. Or rather, nothing that she could see.

With a sigh, she turned and went inside.

# 7

All she knew about Macquarie was that he was a large man, over sixty, and Australian. But when she arrived at the terrace of the Sporting Club, next to the open-air swimming pool and the sea washing over rocks just a few yards beyond, the man waving to her looked more like a farmer than an airline pilot. Tall, heavily-built, weather-beaten, he towered over the little café table as he stood to greet Clemency.

'G'day, Miss Green. What will you have?'

His hand was rough, his grip very strong, but as he gestured to the waiter and ordered Clemency some coffee, chatting about her flight over, she could sense his natural kindliness.

'You'll find it all a bit of a shock. But Farzana will look after you. She's on the early flight from Amman so she should be along any minute. Oh, and that reminds me. There's something I should say when it's just the two of us.'

He looked carefully around him, and then leaned forward, as if wanting to signal to every other customer in the bar that he had something confidential to say.

'You're with the Customs Service, then.'

'Yes.'

'Well, that's fine with me. Except for one thing. You see, the crew has to work as a team. If you're checking up on them, that could get in the way, and the safety of the ship and the passengers is my top priority, now and always. When Mr Rossiter said you'd be joining, he said it was the passengers you were interested in, but I wanted to hear it from you.'

'It's just the passengers, Mr Macquarie. If you or anyone else is taking the odd bottle of whisky back to the hotel without declaring it, then it's nothing to do with me.'

He leaned back, satisfied.

'That's fine. I'm not going to tell the others, of course, but if there's anything I can do to help, anything at all, you let me know. You're on the right track, though. Aviation is full of crooks, from the boardroom down. Now, what do you know of the leg you're working on.'

'I'm not even sure I know what a leg is.'

He laughed.

'Fair enough. So, we're flying three routes. Monday and Wednesday is Basra, there and back in the day. Tuesday and Thursday we do the same to Ahmar. We have Friday and Saturday off, then do a run to Nicosia on Sunday, and then we do the whole thing again.

'I'm the Captain, and the First Officer is Mike Stannard. The cabin crew change round a bit, but at the moment you'll be on with Farzana until next Friday, and then Felicity. You'll like them both. We fly out early to avoid the heat, especially for Ahmar, as that's the edge of our range and we have to load up with extra fuel. The hotter the air, the harder it is to take off.

'The only other thing that's different to most other airlines is we don't have many layovers outside Beirut. We go there and we come back. In Ahmar, even the meals we take out frozen in the hold and get 'em out for the flight back. Apart from putting on the fuel and dumping into the honey wagon, it's just like a stop-over on a single flight.

'Honey-wagon?'

Macquarie almost blushed.

'It's where the... you know, the heads... the toilets... empty into.'

'I'll be cleaning those toilets from tomorrow, Mr Macquarie. It's good to know they can be emptied.'

He laughed.

'You never know where you are with the girls. Some of them start off so prim and proper. You'll do all right. Oh, and when we're on duty, it's Captain, and when we're off-duty it's Bill. All right?'

'Yes, so long as it's not Miss Green, but Caroline.'

'Fair enough. I'll say welcome to the team, Caroline.'

His smile was so genuine, that it pained her that even in this she was deceiving him.

'And look, here she is.'

The young woman coming along the terrace looked so much more at home there than Clemency, with her simple sleeveless dress in cream linen, a single thin gold chain around her neck, her blue-black hair cut just as fashionably short as in London. But her welcome was genuine enough.

'I am only sorry I was not here last night,' she said. 'But as we are sharing a room you are free to look everywhere and take whatever you need – lipstick, hairbrush, anything. But I am sorry, I am interrupting.'

She laid her hand on Macquarie's arm, but they were nothing like a couple – more like a doting uncle and a loving niece, and with the extra connection of being members of a small team. Four people working together for long hours, relying on each other's professionalism, then socialising in a foreign place, and back to work the next day, week in, week out.

'I was telling Caroline how aviation is full of shady characters,' Macquarie said, after ordering drinks from the waiter who had floated along in Farzana's wake. 'Nothing is safe unless it's screwed down.'

'The passengers are the worst,' Farzana's voice had a hint of a French accent. Perhaps she too had studied in Paris.

'Too right,' Macquarie said. 'Air travel seems to draw the crooks in like flies to jam. Though some of them you have to take your hat off to. D'you remember the bloke we flew to Tehran? Had his wife and two kids, travelling first class. Lovely family. We heard later he'd paid with traveller's cheques that were dud. He travelled around the whole world for months. Hotels, flights, all hooky. D'you know how he got away with it? He made his own traveller's cheques. Straight up. He invented the name of the bank, designed the cheques, had them printed up professionally, everything. Of course, the signatures on the counterfoil matched up perfectly when he signed the cheques. It took them that long to cotton on to what he was doing.

'Of course, crews are no better. They steal anything they can. Like bloody termites. If you left a plane in an airport for a week, they'd strip it down to the metal. They'd steal the bloody paint off the wings, wouldn't they?'

'It is true,' Farzana said. 'Often it is borrowing. If one plane has something missing or broken, you think it's right to take it from another. If it is from another airline, then so much the better.'

'Farzana here will tell you that I draw the line at taking anything to sell. The odd half-bottle of hooch for a party, then that's perquisites, and crews have done that since day one. But not to flog it off.'

'Some crews strip the plane,' Farzana added. 'Plates, knives, forks, towels. As if they are to be married and must furnish their whole house.'

'They do that too,' Macquarie added. 'You go round for dinner, and the plates all say Pan Am, the cutlery is BOAC, and the food will be steak tournedos pinched from the galley. We poor bloody pilots don't get a look-in.'

'You have your perquisites too, Captain.' She turned to Clemency. 'Pilots are in charge of the freight. If there's room, they may add cargo of their own. Things that are light but worth money if they move quickly. Like fresh flowers. Or fruit,' she added with a glance at Macquarie.

'Like all these things, it's fine at the start, but then they get greedy. You bring a few bags of oranges back to the English winter, give 'em out to your friends, that's one thing. Before you know it, you're shipping a ton at a time for cash. It costs the airline in extra fuel. And if you start fiddling the manifests, it's bloody dangerous. The all-up weight, the way the cargo is placed in the hold, it's all about the trim and the safety of the aircraft. If you have the wrong stuff on paper and try and keep the true numbers in your head, things can go wrong. Any plane I'm the captain of, the cargo goes on the manifest and if anyone doesn't like it they can put in for a transfer.'

There was an edge to Macquarie's words that Clemency didn't understand. As if recognising he'd struck the wrong tone, he plunged into another of his stories.

'There was this BOAC captain, he got himself

a lovely little business importing crayfish from somewhere down in Africa. Cape Town maybe. He had them in tanks so they were still alive. As I heard it, he was doing so well – that place...' he snapped his fingers to help his memory. 'London. Billingsgate. The big fish market. He had a contact there and they couldn't get enough of them. So he's bringing more and more each flight, until one day he hits a tropical storm, the plane's chucked all over the shop, and when he gets to London the ground crew have to report half a ton of water and a hundred crayfish all over the hold.'

'What happened to him?'

'I think he's still flying. Not with BOAC, of course. The thing is, that could have brought the plane down. If the water had got into the electrics, say. That's what I mean about money. It makes 'em forget that your job is to get safely from A to B. That's what you're paid for.'

He waved for more drinks.

'Like I say, I'm not Holy Joe about it. If there's an inch left in a bottle of scent, help yourself. If you want to bring a carpet home, we'll stick it in the hold. You've just got to know where the line is.'

'And don't touch the fuel?' Farzana suggested.

'God, no. One of the Red Air pilots had a great thing going with the ground crew at Sharjah. They underloaded the fuel by fifty gallons on each flight. Then they'd sell it to another airline. You think what you'd make from that, week in, week out. Until one day he's up at 30,000 feet and hits God's own headwind. And he's got no reserve. Too late to turn back, so he's stuck over the Empty Quarter with fifty passengers in a bloody great glider. Now as it happens, he's a good pilot, and half the desert is as hard and flat as a runway, so he puts her down without a scratch. They fly in some extra fuel and take off again. But that could have had a very different ending. He could have been over the mountains, and then they'd have had it. You see what I mean?'

'I won't touch the fuel, I promise,' Clemency said with mock solemnity.

'Mind you don't. Now, I think I'm cooked both sides and ready for a swim. Don't you run off for lunch without me.'

He heaved himself to his feet and set off for the changing rooms.

'We are so lucky that he is our Captain,' Farzana said, as if drawing Clemency into a conspiracy centred on Macquarie, fondness and tolerance and admiration, and protectiveness. She might have said *he is a good man, and you will love him just as I love him.* But there was no need.

'I love your dress,' Clemency said, drawn into being much more forward than usual. 'Is it French?'

'Sadly, no,' Farzana replied. 'In Beirut, everything can be copied for a fraction of the price. Even Courrèges. I will take you to the place, though, as we are now colleagues. After lunch.'

'Will Mr Stannard be joining us?' Clemency asked.

'Oh, no,' she replied, surprised that she should think he might. 'He lives his own life.'

*

After a swim, lunch, and a tour of Beirut, with Clemency overwhelmed by the new sights and sounds, the bustle of the traffic, the energy of the people, it was a relief to return to the Rookery and to think about supper and sleep. Then Farzana came in with a pile of clothes under her chin: her new uniform. Clemency put it on her bed and began rooting through it all.

'Is everything red?'

'It is.'

Tops, tights, gloves – everything was in flaming scarlet. She held up the dress. It was like a tabard, slit to the waist either side, with long lengths of cloth front and back.

'It is very practical,' Farzana said. 'It is much easier to move around and reach up for things than any other uniform I've had. But I don't think that's why Mr Rossiter chose it.'

'I feel like I'm in a pantomime.'

'There is a pocket at the front that is so useful. And it is all wool and cotton, so you can wash it here and it will be dry in the morning.'

'And this is the hat?'

'There's also a headscarf, and if you leave the plane in Doha or Rasin you will want this *abaya*. It goes over everything and then no-one will say filthy things to you.'

'That's a comfort.'

Trying on the hat and draping the long woollen *abaya* over her shoulders was fun, like playing at dressing up. But tomorrow it would be for real. In the morning, her first flight for Red Air, and the first test of her cover; and in the afternoon, returning with the Emir himself on board. With the flight from London, meeting the crew, her doubts about the mission, the inner voice telling her it was going to go horribly wrong, had receded. Now it was back, worse than ever.

'Are you all right, Caroline?'

'I'm fine. I'm just thinking of tomorrow.'

'Don't worry. I will look after you.'

# 8

The minibus came for them just before six in the morning. It was still dark and Clemency was grateful for the *abaya* to keep off the morning chill. On the drive out to the airport – everyone silent at that early hour, before the first coffee of the day – the sun caught the hills and the houses, sending impossibly long shadows from the trees across the road, turning the sky over the sea to the west a mysterious blackberry-purple. It was almost painfully beautiful, and she began to see why Denholm had fallen in love with the country.

Their plane was sitting in the dawn sun on a far corner of the airport, a cluster of vehicles around it – a bowser to fuel it, another truck pumping in water, and a third with a generator to give the plane power until its own engines were turning. A couple of women in long black dresses and headscarves were coming down the steps with rubbish bags in their hands. Clemency guessed they were the ones who set the plane up before each flight with sick bags and cloths for the headrests and scented soap for the toilet. It made her queasy to see how many people were allowed onto the plane, and how isolated it was, standing only a few yards from a rusty chain-link fence and the outside world.

Macquarie was standing under one wing with another man in pilot's uniform, and they were both staring at something. But it must not have been of any great concern, because as soon as he saw Farzana and

Clemency climb out of the crew bus he clapped the other man on the shoulder and they both walked across to greet them.

Mike Stannard turned out to be the very model of a modern pilot, from his crisply ironed shirt and polished shoes to his languid, confident public-school voice, the kind that would come over the PA and reassure the passengers about storms, fires or the loss of a wing. If he were a bit distant with her, that wasn't a problem as far as she was concerned – much better than being eyed up like merchandise.

The only edge he showed was when she called him the co-pilot.

'I prefer to be called the First Officer,' he said. Not nastily; just as if it mattered to him more than she would have expected. But she'd heard that pilots were incredibly conscious of their status.

The flight out was uneventful; though to Clemency, there was far too much to do, and no time to do it before the next task was upon her. The take-off, strapped to the galley jump-seat, was the only quiet time. After that, she was helping the passengers settle themselves, serving the aperitifs, taking orders for lunch, clearing the aperitifs, refilling drinks for the more demanding passengers, reassuring the more nervous, answering the questions of those who had nothing better to do than chat to or chat up their stewardess, then the lunch trays, the main courses, deserts, coffee and liqueurs. She had these back in the serving trolley, and that back in the galley and latched into its place and was thinking she could sit for five minutes and recover, when she saw that Farzana was unlatching the duty-free cart.

'You're joking.'

'We're five minutes behind as it is,' Farzana said.

'Mr Rossiter is very sharp on this. They make so much money on it. But do not worry, and take your time. You must not rush the addition or the currency conversion. If we get it wrong, it is taken from our wages.'

They made their way up the aisle, offering watches, scent, spirits and chocolate to the passengers who weren't already up to their duty-free limit, or who planned to chance it and take in something extra.

Only when that was over did Clemency realise just how much Farzana had covered for her. She'd done rows 1 to 7, leaving 8 to 11 for Clemency. She'd taken the pilots their meals and coffee. And run some errands for Clemency's passengers. And answered Clemency's many questions. All this without seeming to be hurried or flustered.

'I don't know how you do it.'

'Practice,' Farzana said, disposing of the last of the coffee, then closing up the galley hatches. 'Now we need to go through the cabin and clear any last cups. The set-down will start in a couple of minutes, and the seatbelt and no smoking signs go on. We have to check that carefully. But watch out for the men in Row 9. They will say they cannot work the belt, and have you leaning over to help, and their hands will be where they should not be.'

She took out the belt they used for the safety demonstration.

'Have this in your pocket. You use it to show them, and then make them do it themselves. Or tell them you will get the pilot to do it.'

'I couldn't do that.'

'You will never need to. They do not want trouble. It is their idea of fun.'

As it turned out, the men were all properly belted

up when she reached them and deep in conversation about bars in Kuwait City. Even so, it took her longer than it should to get the cigarettes put out and the tables locked into place and the coats and bags back in their places under the seats or in the overhead racks. All the time she could feel the plane sinking. She only just made it back to her seat as the undercarriage began to come down. She caught a glimpse of the blinding blue of the sea, a boat with a faded red sail, the start of the sandy beach that hardly changed as it became the land, and then a cluster of square white houses and the dome and the lance-like minaret of a mosque.

A few moments later, they were landing smoothly on the airstrip at Ahmar.

*

She stood by the door, already wilting in the intense heat, thanking the passengers, wishing them well, until the last of them was strolling across the concrete towards the tiny terminal. Apart from a couple of hangars, a few low buildings that were probably offices, and a well-worn cargo plane, there was not much to the airfield but dust and flies.

'We have two hours,' Farzana said. 'Do you want to look about? I can prepare the plane.'

'No, I'll stay and help.'

Beyond the airfield were camels and palm trees, Bedouin camps, dates, spices and all the mysteries of the East. But it felt alien; even hostile. She couldn't speak the language, she didn't understand the culture. And somewhere out there was Petrov. The thought scared her. He would have planned everything, have a solid cover and a team around him. She had seen what he was capable of, and had no intention of being caught off guard, or alone.

As she gazed towards the distant walls of the city of Ahmar, a Land-Rover pulled up, and three soldiers in sand-coloured uniforms climbed out. Two wore red berets and were armed with rifles, and the third – an officer – pointed to where he wanted them to stand, and then climbed up the airstairs to where the two women were standing.

'Is Captain Macquarie aboard? He's expecting me. I'm Captain Morris.'

Clemency knew nothing about soldiers, insignia, and the rest; but she could see that the crest on the man's cap seemed to involve eagles and palm trees, not lions and unicorns. He must be an officer in the Emir's own army. The men would be Ahmaris, but there would be good sense – and status – in employing British officers. She was beginning to realise just how much the British called the shots in the Persian Gulf; and how that might be resented.

'Captain Macquarie is at the tower,' Farzana said. 'He will be back soon. He is checking the latest weather reports and filling his flight plan to Beirut.'

Morris nodded, as if used to the ways of pilots.

'My chaps are here to keep an eye on things. Is everything ready for His Excellency?'

Farzana assured him that all was as it should be.

'He'll be arriving at 1pm,' Morris said. 'Once he's on board, you'll load the other passengers. Take off at 1.30pm. Is that right?'

'Yes, that is quite correct,' Farzana replied, unusually formal and starchy. 'If your men need anything – water and so on – they have only to ask.'

'Oh, God, they'll be fine,' Captain Morris said with

a laugh, clattering down the stairs. 'This is a cushy number for them. Nice cool breeze, too.'

Clemency turned to Farzana.

'What's the matter? You look like you've swallowed a wasp.'

'Wasp? Oh, I see.' Her frown gave way to a smile. 'I am sorry. It is a national prejudice. We like the British. They teach us so much. But the further they are from Persia, the more we like them. You see?'

To be fair to him, Morris didn't leave the men and disappear for a refreshing drink in the shade. He stood and chatted with them, then walked around the plane himself for a while, showing considerable interest in the various trucks, cables and pipes.

With the engines and air conditioning switched off, the heat in the cabin was soon rising.

'When it gets hot, you must slow down,' Farzana advised her. 'Keep drinking water and cover your head in the sun. Not that this is truly hot. For that, you must come in August. Or go to the heart of the Empty Quarter.'

'What's that?'

'The great desert we have flown over. It is well-named. There is nothing there. No towns or villages. No water. Like a great sea of sand.'

'I didn't have a chance to look at it.'

'There is not much to see. Sometimes it is sand dunes, and sometimes it is flat, like a dried-up lake. But it is as dangerous as the sea. If the course is wrong, the plane can be lost and never found. That is why I like to fly with Captain Macquarie. He is a very careful pilot. With navigation, with the weather. Everything.'

# 9

They had the plane readied in good time, and just on one o'clock a convoy of cars swept across the tarmac and pulled up by the nose. The old man in white flowing robes who stepped out of the leading car, looking around a little uncertainly, must be the Emir. The elegant woman in traditional dress who took his arm would be his daughter Fatima. A man in a dark European suit and headdress – what Clemency had already learned was called a *keffiyeh* – climbed from the front passenger seat: this would be the Emir's secretary, Hamid. Meanwhile, two men hurried along from the car behind to form the Emir's guard, rifles held casually, long curved knives at their belts.

The Emir gazed around the cabin, expressionless, taking in every detail. Farzana waited patiently until he had adjusted to this new setting – although he must have flown on the company's planes many times before – and he chose the seat by the window and closest to the door. His daughter sat beside him and began to talk to him in a low voice. The guards looked around warily and then consented to having their rifles taken from them by Farzana and put in the locker by the toilet. One of them took a seat behind the Emir, on the aisle, and the other took the jump seat that faced backwards into the cabin. Both sat rigid, their hands on their daggers.

This done, Clemency signalled to the despatcher at the door of the terminal to let the passengers through.

They straggled across the tarmac, most of them carrying small bags, newspapers or magazines. There were about thirty of them, all men, mostly Europeans or Americans. None of them looked at all suspicious or out of place. Then, with a surge of relief, she realised that the one at the back, in a dark suit, bareheaded, his eyes hidden behind sunglasses, was David. She was no longer alone.

She welcomed them all on board, checking their boarding passes. When it was David's turn, he paused for a moment.

'Can you tell me when we'll be in Beirut?' he asked.

'We're due in at half past five,' she replied, very cool and professional. 'If there's anything you need, you just have to call.'

'I'll be sure to do that,' he said with a smirk, then moved on into the cabin. His seat was the first on the right, 11C. It gave him a view of the whole cabin. She wondered how he had arranged this.

The first of the four engines began to turn over. Clemency turned to settling the other passengers. She took their jackets to hang up, running her hand over them for anything concealed as she did so; and helped them stow their bags under their seats, giving each one a surreptitious check to see if it were unusually heavy. She said something to each one, asking how their day was or insisting they call her if there were anything she could do to make their flight more comfortable, and the way each one responded seemed absolutely normal, whether friendly or offhand.

This done, she went to tell Farzana that all was ready and watched as she handed back some paperwork to the ground crew. Then Farzana closed the door and swung the heavy lever to lock it into place. It had the finality of the closing of a tomb. If there were hijackers on board, or a bomb, then there was no longer any escape.

They walked back to their seats by the galley and Clemency found some comfort in the steel of the bulkhead at her back, though she knew that if disaster struck, it would provide little protection.

The plane began to taxi to its take-off position, and for a while Clemency could convince herself that all was well, that this was no worse than taking a ride in a bus. But then they turned to line up on the runway, and the noise increased as the engines came to full power, so that the plane shuddered, held back only by the brakes. As soon as they began to roll forward, she realised that it was all wrong, that she didn't want to be there – no, *couldn't* be there, would have to stop the plane and get off. It took an effort of will not to unbuckle herself and try and open the door. It was hard to breathe, and she felt as if she'd eaten something poisonous, with sweat on her brow and a sick feeling in her stomach.

The rumble of the wheels stopped and the ground fell away. At once Clemency thought of the altitude, the idea that somewhere on the plane was a bomb, ready to explode as soon as they reached the predetermined height. It might be in the baggage hold, or in the tail section behind the galley. She prayed it would be there, because then it would all be over before she knew what had happened.

A minute passed, then another.

Farzana stood up, took the handset and announced that the passengers could now undo their seat belts and smoke. Clemency remembered this was her cue to start readying the meals, just like on the flight out. But she worked with only half her mind; the other half expecting the skin of the plane to bloom apart and for her to be spilled into the blue. She struggled with the thought that the last thing she might do in her life was to arrange some salmon and cheese puffs on a plate.

Then she began taking orders for drinks from the passengers, and soon forgot the idea of a bomb in the more immediate challenge of her job. She even greeted David as if he were just another passenger, until she was reminded by his sardonic smile.

'I'd like a vodka martini,' he said. 'Two parts vermouth to one of Russian vodka. Over ice. An olive. Stirred, not shaken.'

'Of course, sir,' she said, wondering how he could find the courage to make a joke of their situation. 'And you, sir?' she added to the man to David's right, determined to show that she could be the perfect stewardess. But the man, clutching the seat handles and staring fixedly at the ground, as if praying he might one day return safely to it, waved her away.

With the drinks served, she realised they were at their cruising altitude. No bomb. But for twenty minutes she had done nothing to try and spot a hijacker or an assassin.

She walked back down the aisle, dispensing smiles and checking that they all had everything they wanted, but also trying to see if anything were out of place. But they all looked the part, down to the crew cuts, the sunburn and the gallantry. Surely you wouldn't start trying to chat up the stewardess on a plane you proposed to hijack.

At least Vaughn's idea, that a stewardess could examine passengers in a way no one else could, stood up to the test of reality. She could talk to them, see if they were relaxed or fidgety, had their nose in a magazine or were showing an unhealthy interest in the flight deck. And by the time she'd served the first course, she was sure that they were going to be all right. No-one gave the slightest grounds for suspicion. Even the four Arabs on board – and surely it was more likely that Ahmaris would lead any hijack – looked like who they said they were: two going to a training course for geologists in London; and two for business in Beirut; which would no doubt be mixed with a dash of pleasure, judging by their eagerness to know when the plane would arrive.

In fact, the only suspicious character was David, with his pale skin with the first flush of sunburn that revealed a new arrival in the Gulf; his dark suit; his watchfulness.

*

Two more hours, the meal served and cleared away, and Clemency was in the galley, preparing coffee and remembering her briefing. The distance to Beirut was around 1,100 miles and would take the Viscount about four hours. Most of that was over the empty tracts of the Saudi desert, only in contact with the rest of the world when they reported their position by radio. It was only in the last half hour as they began the set-down towards Beirut that they would appear on the radar screens in Jordan and Lebanon.

'I wondered if I could have some more of your excellent coffee?'

It was David, leaning against the bulkhead by the galley. She poured him a cup and passed it to him with a cool look.

'It's cover,' he said quietly. 'What would a young single British man do on a long flight? He'd chat up the stewardesses.'

'Would he?'

'And I expect – she being bored as well – she might go along with it.'

'Might she?' Clemency turned away to tidy up some spilt milk.

'It would even explain why he always asks for the same seat. Next to the galley. More chance for a bit of flirting.'

She didn't look up. No-one could overhear them. The noise of the engines and the air rushing past at over 300 miles an hour saw to that.

'These orders are from London, I suppose?'

'A bit of local initiative, actually,' he said with a grin.

'You should go back to your seat now, Mr Fletcher,' she said briskly, taking the cup from him. 'The Captain will be putting the seat belt sign on in a minute.'

He went off amiably and she finished tidying up, then went through the cabin, picking up any last cups or glasses. But her encounter had not gone unnoticed.

'Trouble?' Farzana asked. 'Only I saw 11C talking to you.'

'He was bored. He won't be a problem.'

'I hope you are right, but…'

She turned away with a half-hidden smile.

'What is it?'

'Nothing, nothing… Only our esteemed first officer was using the washroom and saw him with you and I do not think he was pleased.'

Farzana's eyes were full of mischief as she set off down the aisle. Clemency watched her with half her mind, distracted by the thought that Stannard, despite hardly having spoken five words to her, might be interested in her. It was a complication she didn't need, she told herself severely, however much self-satisfaction it might also bring.

The descent into Beirut was routine. As soon as it began, Clemency felt all the stress and tension melt away. In theory, a bomb could be set to explode on the descent, perhaps to divert attention away from Ahmar. But she knew this flight at least would arrive safely. With the final preparations and checks, it was almost too soon that they were touching down and the engines were thrown into reverse to slow their speed. They made their way to their arrival gate, and the usual cluster of vehicles drew up, including a protocol officer from the Lebanese Ministry of Foreign Affairs to welcome the Emir to his country. While Farzana helped the Emir and his entourage out through the front to their waiting cars, Clemency disembarked the passengers through the rear door. As he passed, David winked.

'I hope you enjoyed your flight,' she said in the same pleasant, unmeaning way she had used for the other passengers.

'Yes, thank you. I'm sure I'll be back.'

# 10

There was to be a regular meeting when the Emir was in Beirut to review progress and report anything significant back to London. Denholm had rented a flat in one of the sea-front apartment blocks, where there were plenty of Westerners coming and going and no particular sense of community, no-one to ask questions about the new residents in apartment 412 or wonder where they were for the other six days of the week.

David opened the door, pulled a face at her and then led her to where Farringdon was seated on a sofa, a briefcase open beside him and files spread around. He was wearing an open-neck shirt and a cravat as a concession to having left Whitehall.

'You remember Miss White?' David said.

'Yes, of course,' the man replied with no obvious enthusiasm.

She took the empty seat next to Denholm. The room was spacious, with one whole wall of windows giving onto a balcony overlooking the sea. It was furnished with faint good taste: low leather sofas, unobtrusive art, an abstract sculpture. The burnished copper coffee pot and the Bedouin carpet hanging on the wall were all that suggested that they were in the Middle East and not Hong Kong or San Francisco.

'Well, one flight out of twelve ticked off,' Farringdon said, to start them off. 'David, how did it go?'

At first it was interesting to hear David's view of

the day, and she was pleased that he included praise for her own hard work – *I thought Miss White played her part admirably* – but it soon became clear that she was there not to speak but to listen, and then, perhaps, to be given instructions. When David had finished, Farringdon turned to Denholm.

'What about the Beirut airport side of things?'

This dragged on too, with Farringdon cross-questioning him about who was guarding the plane each night, and how access to the airport was controlled, and who his contacts were at the Ministry of Internal Security. Even Denholm, usually so polite and helpful, began to look put out by the interrogation. It was as if the man from MI5 could not believe that anyone from Six could organise physical security.

The meeting wound up and David engineered it to leave at the same time as Clemency, and it was natural for him to suggest dinner. She guessed he was at a loose end in Beirut. A quiet night in his hotel room with an improving book was not his style.

He took her to a restaurant that one of the staff at the Residency in Ahmar had recommended to him. It didn't compare to the place that she had gone to with Denholm on her first night in Beirut, and she was glad she wasn't paying the ridiculous prices. But clearly David needed to relax, and splash a little money, from the way he was knocking back the wine.

'God, you're lucky being here,' he said. 'Ahmar is such a bloody hole. The Residency crowd are decent enough but there's nothing to do there. Imagine a village in the Welsh valleys on a Sunday, only it's too hot to move and there isn't even a male voice choir.'

'It can't be that bad,' she replied.

'It most certainly can.' He launched into a

diatribe on Ahmar's failings, and the laziness and untrustworthiness of its inhabitants from the Vizier down.

'I've seen a bit of the Emir, and he's a decent old bird, but the sons are a horror show. Abdullah is a crashing bore. I mean, I like cars, but there are limits. You can be with him for an hour or more, and he just bangs on and on about Armstrong-Siddeleys and Lucas carburettors, and does so in the English of 1924. Everything's topping or marvellous. It's excruciating. The only good thing is that I'm absolutely convinced he's not the one behind the plot. He's too damned dull.'

'That's something.'

'Mohammed is simply rude. Lots of snide remarks about Britain's imperial mission. It just goes to show what a university education does to these people. He's sly, though. This mild socialism he preaches – it's all about how the lot of the ordinary Ahmaris needs to improve, as if he cared – it's a great cover for out and out Communism. He's definitely in with the Soviets. One of his hangers-on has been in Moscow.'

'Do you really think he's planning to kill his own father?'

'Look at them shooting the King of Jordan after Friday prayers. Or the King of Iraq, pulled out of his palace and butchered by the mob. Out here, there's always violence in the background. Maybe it's the heat.'

He finished his wine.

'What about you? Have you heard anything?'

It was said as an afterthought; and although she'd wanted to share her own impressions, she wasn't sure if now were the right time.

After the meal, they danced for a while. The band was playing the Beach Boys and Roy Orbison, but as if they were reading it from sheet music and had never heard the originals; and David turned out to be surprisingly stiff and clumsy. So she suggested a walk, and they strolled along the Corniche, enjoying the warmth of the night, the slow wash of the sea on the beach, the lights and the chatter from the bars and restaurants; people enjoying themselves and not worrying about politics and intrigue. It was relaxing with David so reassuring at her side. Both in Beirut and on the plane, it was impossible to imagine coming to any harm when he was there to look after her.

She thought of saying some of this; but that might not be wise. After all, he was clearly as interested in girls as any other young man and she didn't want to seem to encourage him. Instead, she said she ought to be getting back to the Rookery.

They parted at the door; she got away without being kissed; but the way he'd shaken hands, lingering just a little, gazing just a little too intently, showed her she'd need to be careful.

*

The next day Clemency flew to Amman and back twice. The shorter flight time meant that serving and collecting the meals was even more of a rush and by the final flight Clemency was dead on her feet.

'How's it going?' Felicity asked, appearing at her side in the galley.

'I'm so tired. I don't know how you manage.'

'It's a knack. The first week's always the worst. Everything's new. And the atmosphere too. You know, the cabin is not fully pressurised. It's like being up a mountain.'

She started pulling the meals out of the oven and dropping them onto the trays.

'It's terribly dry, too. Worse than the Sahara, they say. You have to keep drinking water or you start to get a headache. Moisturiser, too. Hands and face, and even your neck. Take as much as you like from the toilets. We pinch it anyway at the end of the flight.'

'Really?'

'One of the perks. There have to be some.'

'Is it that bad?'

'No, it's a wonderful job. But stews shouldn't ever have to pay for food and drink. Not when you have them on board to give out for free. It's the same when we go out. I don't think I've paid for a drink since I joined Red Air. You should come with me one evening.'

Since she'd first moved to London, five years before, Clemency had met many Felicitys. For them, life was a quest for fun and for the latest thing – music, clothes, clubs, drinks. It could seem shallow, and it wasn't Clemency's world, though she liked all those too. There was the little girl act too, the passivity, the wide innocent eyes, all about letting the boys think they were making all the decisions. Clemency only had to see Felicity at work to know she was far from stupid: but on the ground, men would underestimate her, perhaps say things in her presence that they would assume would go over her head. Felicity might know a lot more than she let on.

'I'd really like that,' Clemency said. 'How about when I'm back from Ahmar?'

# 11

On the Thursday they flew the Emir and his entourage back to Ahmar. He looked drained, as if tired by the journey and the medical treatment, but the flight was without incident. It was also less tense, at least for Clemency. Despite Farringdon's concerns about security in Beirut, she was convinced the danger lay in Ahmar.

Soon Clemency's life settled into a pattern. The shuttle bus to the airport in the cool of the dawn; preparing the plane. Then the morning flight, two hours to turn around, refuel, prepare the plane, and then they were on the way back, bumpy at first with the heat coming off the desert, but then climbing to the smoother air and the long, wearying hours of serving the passengers. They'd land in the late afternoon, giving her a chance to relax, have a swim, go out for a meal or a drink, and then the next morning she would do it all over again.

One break from the routine came on the third of the round trips to Ahmar. Each time they landed there, Mike Stannard would go into the town and return laden with crates of fruit, bags of coffee or sacks of nuts to go into the hold. Farzana, making mischief, suggested to Stannard that he was being most unfair in not showing Clemency the town of Ahmar. He looked put out, but could hardly refuse; nor could Clemency, though she had no desire to spend time in his company.

But somehow, once the passengers were disembarked, Farzana was there helping Clemency with her *abaya* and headscarf, and Stannard was there with the jeep that was to drive him to the souk.

They sped along the track, past the old fort now used as a rest-house, and then the walls of Ahmar came into view through the heat haze, the same honey-gold as the desert around them. There were date gardens to either side of the track, a train of camels, boys leading laden donkeys, flocks of sheep or goats herded by young girls with sticks. It was quite different from Beirut; no trace of Western culture, no adverts for Cinzano or Marlboro, no cars, everyone in traditional dress, the women all wearing the veil.

They parked in a kind of square with a well at its centre, and Stannard led her up a steep alley, with shallow steps, the houses close on each side, seeming to lean towards each other so that the sky was no more than a slit of blue high overhead. Clemency was glad to have Stannard at her side, though he said nothing. She was conscious that her face was not covered, and there were glances, hard to read, from some of the men she passed.

'I suppose it would be a shame not to see the town, when you're so close,' he said in the end, as if conscious he was being rude. 'I'm sorry we can't look around, though.'

The souk was next to the creek around which the town was built, and on a much grander scale than she had imagined. There were row upon row of stalls, each piled with produce of every imaginable kind. If you ignored the dust and the heat, and the flies that crawled over everything, the display – particularly the grapes and the dates – were mouth-watering. There were traders selling bolts of cloth, carpets, household goods too, tools, even nails and screws. She was taken with the sacks of spices that wrapped her in scent as she passed; but Stannard ignored these, and made for one particular stall near the quay, where a sour-looking man in a striped robe and a greasy cap greeted Stannard with no great warmth. Clemency had expected a theatrical amount of haggling, but in no time the deal was sealed and the money handed over, and the merchant signalled to some underlings to carry the crates of fruit back down to the jeep.

It was a squeeze to get it all on board, and Clemency ended up perched on top of a sack of pistachio nuts. She had to hang on tight as they sped back through the narrow streets towards the gate.

'How much do you make from all this?' she shouted out to him.

'It depends on what's in season and what's in demand,' he replied. 'It probably works out at about ten dollars a crate.'

It was much less than she had expected, and she wondered why he bothered. Perhaps it wasn't the money, but the sense of getting something for nothing. Or putting one over on Rossiter.

They drew up in front of the plane and the driver began to hump the crates over to the forward cargo door, while Stannard climbed inside to make sure they were all stowed safely. She called up her thanks to him, then went into the cabin, where Farzana was still preparing the plane for the return flight. She realised she'd been away for less than an hour, and felt a little ridiculous, particularly when Farzana asked her what she had seen.

'Hardly anything,' she replied. 'Not the mosque, or

the royal palace, or the famous walls. You'll have to tell me what else I missed.'

'I cannot say,' Farzana replied. 'You forget that I must not leave the airfield. I do not have a visa.'

'That's a shame,' Clemency replied, embarrassed to have forgotten that Farzana was Persian. But she seemed to think the whole thing funny.

'What I regret most is that I cannot see Mr Stannard negotiating with the traders. That would amuse me greatly. You must tell me everything.'

The Emir's son Mohammed joined the return flight but, frustratingly, he was seated at the front of the plane and was greeted and looked after by Farzana. Clemency only spoke to him twice – one to fetch him another glass of mint tea, and once to ask him to fold up his table before they came into land, and he was offhand about the first and annoyed about the second. But beyond seeing that he was arrogant, none of it helped.

That was the problem with her role in the mission. Even if the Russians were involved, the heart of the conspiracy lay in Ahmar. But she never met or spoke to any Ahmaris, or any Arabs, except to offer them drinks or tell them when the plane was due to land. Perhaps it didn't matter. Her job was simply to monitor the passengers. But her deep-down fear was that Vaughn and Farringdon and even David were no closer to the people than she was.

*

The next day they were rostered for a reposition; another piece of jargon that Felicity explained was a flight to put a plane in the right airport, but which carried no passengers. The pilots had to carry out all the same checks and inspections; but for Felicity and Clemency, all they had to do was to climb aboard and sit back in the first-class seats.

'This is the life,' Felicity said, stretching out and kicking off her shoes. 'Four meals to serve, not fifty. No whining children. No vomit. No idiot questions or hands up the skirt.'

'We won't know what to do with ourselves.'

'I will. I'm going to sleep the whole way.'

She was as good as her word; but Clemency found the unexpected sense of freedom too stimulating. She didn't mind brewing coffee for Macquarie and Stannard, leaving Felicity to snore gently.

As always, coming onto the flight deck was a thrill. Instead of the glimpse of the sky through the portholes, here it was spread in front of them, and rushing at them at over three hundred miles an hour.

'How's the weather?' she asked.

'Good as you'd want,' Stannard replied casually. 'Clear all the way to Riyadh.'

'And the return?'

Usually she wouldn't have bothered them in this way; but it was all part of the holiday mood.

'We'll be fine. At least, up here we will. I'm afraid you and Felicity are going to have some turbulence in the cabin. Fifty oil men who haven't had a drink or a girl in three months.'

'Good thing I know judo,' Clemency said.

'Oh, do you? Well, at least I'm forewarned. But it's all part of my theory that there's a lot of hidden depths to you, Caroline.'

Clemency decided not to say anything more. Stannard was too smart, too cynical, to run the risk of flirting with him.

'They're all right,' Macquarie said indulgently. 'Just tell'em if they play up you'll lock the drinks cupboard and throw the key out of the window. That'll shut them up. No offence to your charms, Caroline, but what these boys will want more than anything else in the world is a beer.'

'All this talk of drink,' Stannard said with mock irritation. 'I'm off for a Jimmy Riddle. You got it, Bill?'

'I have it. No rush if you want to have a snooze. Miss Green here will keep me awake.'

'Fair enough.'

Stannard squeezed past and out of the cockpit and Clemency found herself being invited to take his place.

'Best seat in the house,' Macquarie said. 'Enjoy it while you can.'

She settled in. The seat was still warm from Stannard's body, which was an odd feeling of intimacy with a man she disliked; but soon she was enjoying the sense of authority that came from being surrounded by so many dials, switches, levers and lights.

'I suppose everyone asks what they all do?'

'I suppose you're right. Truth is, you don't need very many of them, even to fly a ship like this. All you want to know is, how high you are, which way you're pointing, and how fast you're going. Everything else is just a detail.'

'If you say so.'

'Height is this one here. Speed is here. And the compass is here. For the truly idle – and that includes yours truly – you put the heading, airspeed and height you want in here, press this button, and the ship flies itself. Automatic pilot.'

'You don't have to hold the controls, then?'

'You don't have to be in the cockpit. Put the right

numbers in and it will take you to Riyadh. Of course, it can't quite land the ship. Yet. I'm sure that'll come and then we pilots'll be redundant and it'll just be you stewardesses on board. Or maybe they'll put vending machines in and let the passengers do the work for themselves.'

'That sounds rather sinister.'

'Don't worry. It'll never happen. The passengers depend on having my reassuring presence at the controls. Soon Rossiter will work out that pilots with firm chins and chiselled good looks, and maybe just a few crinkly lines round the eyes and a bit of grey at the temples, they're the ones the passengers want to fly with. It'll be like stewardesses: we'll be recruited for our good looks and charming personalities.

'You're laughing at me.'

'It's quite true. Then we'll spend our time striding up and down the cabin looking like Cary Grant, and you'll be up front checking the robot hasn't blown a fuse.'

'Well, female pilots won't be coming anytime soon.'

'That's my point. Plenty of women can fly just as well as any man. I saw it in the war. Some hot-shot pilot would bring a plane back riddled with holes and half the wing hanging off and get himself a VC. Then a chit of a girl would get behind the controls and fly it off to the factory to be repaired. No lack of skill. Or courage.'

'Well, in wartime…'

'It's all run by the advertising blokes,' he went on. 'They've decided you need pretty young stewardesses such as yourself, and grey-haired types like me up front. But I could serve tea and coffee just as well as you, and you could fly the plane just as well as me.

It's what the customers want that matters. No women pilots, and no male crew in the cabin.'

'Do you really think women can fly as well as men?'

'I'll show you. Put your hands on the controls. No, like this. Just rest them lightly. Here and here. Got it?'

He leaned over and flipped a switch.

'There. You're flying the plane.'

'You're joking.'

'Dead serious. Now, try moving the yoke very gently to port. See?'

Almost before she could believe it, the plane was following her commands and the nose was moving very slowly to the left.

'Then back again. Good. Now the same to starboard.'

She followed his instructions for several more minutes, and began to enjoy herself.

'I wouldn't do this with passengers on board, of course,' Macquarie said. 'They'd have my licence. Now, take the two levers to your right and edge them forward about half an inch. You hear the noise change? And feel the pull on the stick? The greater the speed, the greater the lift over the wings, and so the ship wants to go up.'

There was more of this, as Macquarie went through the basics of flight control, explaining it in his slow Australian drawl as if it were how to change a tyre or shear a sheep.

'Now landing is the tricky bit. Get that wrong and it hurts. The secret is, you slow down by cutting back on the engine revs, and as you lose speed you have to make more lift from the wings with the flaps – that wheel to your side. Once you're on the glide path to the runway, it's easing off the power and putting down the flaps. First five degrees, then ten, then twenty. And taking off? Just the same, only the other way round. Lots of flaps, lots of power, and up you go. Nothing to it.'

It was fun to learn, to play at being a pilot, but being taken seriously was a deeper satisfaction. She felt for the first time as if she were on a team, a kind of junior partner to Macquarie and Stannard.

But the feeling didn't last once Stannard was back, with his sour comments about women drivers who were all over the sky and making him spill his coffee.

Macquarie said nothing as she slipped out of Stannard's seat; just winked. Even if he were on her side, it didn't do to fall out with your first officer. Not good for the safety of the ship, as Macquarie would say. With him, that always came first.

*

Another week, another round trip to Ahmar ticked off, and once again they met in the flat overlooking the sea. Denholm was away in the North on some mysterious task of his own. David passed on the latest thoughts of the Residency in Ahmar. What opposition there was to the Emir's rule came from some of the more extreme clerics on one side, who resented the creeping Westernisation of the country and wanted him to turn back the clock; and the progressives, who wanted him to introduce full-blown democracy, hopefully with themselves leading the new parties.

'What about the Army?' Farringdon asked. 'Who can count on their support?'

'If you recall, sir, it has British officers. The Emir has a personal bodyguard of about twenty men. If there's any fighting, it will be small-scale. But even that could be problematic. It's not a very big place,

Ahmar, and the last thing the new Emir will want is some kind of blood feud. He'll keep it in the family, as you might say. Hence the advantage of the old Emir being disposed of away from Ahmar and with no actual fighting. That's why this *Shura* is so important. The conservatives – and that's almost everyone in Ahmar – won't want to rock the boat if he does name a successor, and his personal bodyguard will transfer their allegiance.'

'What about the younger bother, Suleiman? I don't want us to lose sight of him completely.'

'He's spending a lot of time with the clerics, rather ostentatiously, as if he's trying to become their man, or gaining their support. But we – the Residency – can't quite square this aeroplane plot with a bunch of medievally-minded priests. Equally, there's not that much more to point at Mohammed. There's no significant Communist presence in Ahmar.'

They wrangled about this for a while, and there was nothing that Clemency could contribute. The previous week they'd told her to engage the Emir's wife, Fatima, in conversation, because the Residency had no contacts in the palace *harim*. Unfortunately, she was Persian and chattered away with Farzana at every chance she had, and Clemency was left to deal with her own passengers at the back of the plane.

'Oh, I had the files on the crew sent out from London,' Farringdon said. 'Not much in them. Macquarie's service record with the RAAF, their pilot training reports, some stuff from the Inland Revenue for Stannard. By the way, Miss Felicity Clarke is in Debrett's, would you believe? She's the niece of the Marquis of Haileybury. I suppose that puts her in the clear,' he added with a chuckle.

'Do you want me to make contact with either of the pilots, sir?' David asked. 'Stannard's about my age. I don't think it would look out of place. I could ask him about night spots in Beirut – something like that.'

'Let's leave that in reserve,' Farringdon replied. 'Best not to draw too much attention to you. And we have Miss White covering that. Anything to add, by the way?'

'If any of them is involved, then it's Stannard. And it would be for money, not ideology.'

'Really? Is there something concrete we should follow up on? Or is this feminine intuition?'

His tone was infuriating, but what stung the most was that it was true she was using her intuition. That, and Felicity telling her about an evening she'd spent with Mike at the casino, and how at home he'd seemed at the tables, the chips piled in front of him, playing for high stakes.

'He's very reserved,' she explained. 'He doesn't join in with the rest of the crew. He's the only one who spends any time away from the plane when it's in Ahmar, so there would be more opportunity to contact a local GRU cell.'

'I see from the file that he's been at the airline for over a year, so it would be an odd coincidence if he were also a Soviet agent. They could hardly have known that he'd be of any use to them flying that route, could they?'

His tone was cutting. For a moment, no-one said anything, and Clemency kept her gaze on the brass coffee pot.

As usual, she and David went out for dinner afterwards. At first, they had spent most of their time with their heads close together, discussing the mission. But with each passing week, there was less to say. Clemency had began to think of her return to the Embassy in Bern. She was only there in the hope of luring Petrov into a trap, and if the plot against the Emir was no more than a rumour, then she was wasting her time.

But for David, the end of the mission couldn't come soon enough.

'It's the waiting I can't stand. It's all right for you. You have things to do. I just have to sit there for four hours. And it isn't only on the plane. There's sod-all to do in Ahmar. The Residency people have that all taped. So I have a week of waiting until it's time for the flight again.'

He did look a bit frayed, but when she suggested he stay over in Beirut for a change of scene, he waved the idea away.

'I'm just letting off steam,' he said. 'It's fine really.'

She wondered. He was drinking far too much, and there was a patch of eczema on the back of his hand. But she sensed that if she pushed it, it would only make him angry. If he was anxious, at least it showed he was still taking his role seriously, still keyed-up in case someone tried to hijack the plane, and that was good for them all.

# 12

Clemency's suspicions about Mike Stannard might have been brushed aside by Farringdon and treated with amusement by David, but Clemency still felt something didn't add up.

On the next flight to Beirut, she made a point of paying no attention to Mike or to his consignment of fruit. Once they were on the ground, and the passengers sent on their way, she left the crew room and hurried to the café on the roof of the terminal. As she'd hoped, there was a good view from the terrace of Zebra Peter sitting outside the maintenance area. She bought a coffee and leaned on the railing, as if enjoying the afternoon sun.

After a while, a truck drove up and three men got out: Stannard, another pilot and a man in brown overalls. They soon had the cargo door open and the third man, older but strongly-built, climbed in and began manoeuvring the crates to the edge of the hatch. The he jumped down and carried them to the back of the van. The two pilots stood watching. It all took less than five minutes. Stannard closed the cargo door and they drove off along the perimeter road. She followed its progress behind several hangers and warehouses until it drew up by another plane. The whole process was reversed, with the crates going into the forward hold. She didn't know what kind of plane it was, beyond it having four engines and seeming to be a little larger than Zebra Peter; but she could recognise the stylised bird on the tail fin: British Falcon.

She went down through the terminal to take the shuttle bus into the city. She'd learned nothing, except that Stannard's contact was a pilot with British Falcon; which is what she'd have expected anyway, given that they were sister airlines, both run by Rossiter. She was no nearer knowing whether Stannard was planning to slip a weapon into the fruit on a future flight; or if the trips to the *souk* to buy them were cover for contacts with the conspirators.

But it was the only lead she had.

On an impulse, she went back into the airport. As Peter had instructed her long ago, she always carried enough money to, as he put it, *make things happen*. Armed with this, she went to one of the boutiques and bought an *abaya* and a scarf, hardly haggling over the price, and then put them on in the toilets. She added some heavy eyeliner that made her appear less like her usual self, and found the look surprisingly appealing. Up close, Stannard would recognise her; but she didn't want to be close; only to follow him when he left the airport. If there was more to his exchange with the other pilot than melons and avocados, then he might be on his way to a clandestine meeting – just as Clemency went to a meeting with Farringdon and the others after each flight up from Ahmar.

She waited to one side until Stannard emerged and climbed onto the bus and found a seat towards the back. She went aboard to sit where she would see him if he passed, but where he would only see the back of her head in the enclosing scarf. She had her story ready – that she was visiting a friend who lived in one of the Muslim districts and wanted to blend in – but in the event she could follow him off the bus at the city centre without being noticed.

Stannard set off from the square, away from the docks, weaving through the traffic and the crowds of shoppers and the men delivering baskets of bread and crates of fruit to the cafés and stores. She had to hurry to keep him in sight and was almost run down by a youth on a moped on the corner by the Rivoli. Stannard turned into a narrow side-street but she was more confident of her disguise because the passers-by didn't look at her twice. She was no longer a Western woman in this Eastern city.

The passage narrowed and passed under an arch and into another street. They were climbing and the shops were left behind. It was residential now, large houses set back from the street behind high iron railings and screened by poplars or palms. There was still the occasional car, a boy with a donkey, a man cycling past with great dignity despite carrying a large brown suitcase on the handlebars; but Stannard and she were the only pedestrians.

He paused on the corner and looked both ways to cross the street. She slowed her pace a little and stayed on her side of the road. But moments later, her pursuit was over. He stopped at the next house and rang the bell. The gate clicked open and he went inside. The villa was hard to make out behind the high wall, and she couldn't tell if it were a private residence or being used as some kind of office. She risked walking to the end of the road, completing a loop and passing by a few minutes later. A discreet brass plate on the wall announced that it was the Clinic Sassine, under the direction of one Dr Albert Precout.

There was nothing else she could think to do. It

was time to return to the Rookery before her makeshift disguise let her down. Probably this visit to a clinic would mean nothing. Perhaps Mike had an ingrowing toenail. He might even be there for the medical check that all pilots had to complete every six months.

It began to dawn on her how reckless she had been. The mission depended on keeping her cover, and how could she have explained to Mike what she was doing there? She could hear Peter ticking her off, about needing to stick to your own job and trust your colleagues to do theirs. Then, with her mind full of recriminations, she missed the entrance to the passage that led back towards the main square. She was almost at the corniche before she regained her bearings, and she was hot and tired and irritable and very hungry by the time she made it back to the Rookery.

She could imagine David's amused, superior expression if she told him about this futile adventure. Not that she ever would.

*

Clemency took a shower in the rackety bathroom at the top of the house, not minding that the trickle of water was lukewarm after the heat of the day. She came back to her room to find Farzana looking critically at the *abaya* she had bought at the airport and thrown carelessly on her bed.

'You should have told me you wished to buy one,' she said severely. 'I hope you did not pay too much.'

'What's wrong with it?'

'The fabric is cheap, and the embroidery is very bad. A machine. A bad machine. This is the kind of thing they sell in the airport,' she added dismissively.

'I got sick of being stared at,' Clemency said. But this only made Farzana seemed more puzzled.

'In Beirut? Perhaps if you go to the old town…'

Farzana indulged her habit of not letting a topic go, until Clemency distracted her by proposing they go out to eat rather than struggle with the ancient stove in the basement kitchen. She suggested the restaurant to which Denholm had taken her on her first night in Beirut, thinking it would be a good place for two young women who did not want to be bothered by stray men. The owner welcomed Clemency and asked after her uncle, and of course Farzana would not stop until she knew all about him – or thought she did.

But her boundless curiosity had one advantage: she was as happy to answer questions as to ask them. Clemency steered her onto the subject of Mike Stannard, though this meant some probing about Clemency's mysterious admirer in Seat 11C, and whether Mike had cause to be jealous. But at last Clemency could ask how it was that Alec Rossiter, who seemed to know everything about his airline, could be ignorant of Mike's fruit business.

'Ignorant?' Farzana's eyes were wide in surprise. 'Of course he knows of it. But he can say nothing.'

'Why?'

'Ah, but there is a mystery, you see. I believe that Mr Stannard knows something about Mr Rossiter. Perhaps embarrassing, perhaps damaging. I am sure that Mr Stannard would not see it as blackmail, but maybe he has let Mr Rossiter know that he knows.'

'What on earth could it be?' Clemency asked invitingly. Farzana leaned closer, resting her hand on Clemency's sleeve.

'I was so close to discovering,' she said. 'One day,

there was a question of checking the serial number of a visa. For Kuwait, I think. It was all a rush and no-one else was about so he took me into his office and he handed me my file to find what I needed. But he gave me the wrong file. It was Mike's.'

'And?'

'I only had a moment, and then I realised it was not mine. Then he snatched it back from me. But I had still seen.'

Farzana was delighting in drawing out the story, and now stopped to sip her wine, and then dab her lips demurely with her napkin.

'What was it?' Clemency hissed.

'A bank transfer. For many thousands of dollars. Far more than he would earn in a month.'

'You think Alec is being blackmailed?'

Farzana drew back in mock horror.

'I think nothing. This is only what I saw. But believe me, there is some mystery between them.'

That was all she learned. But that night, Clemency found it hard to sleep. She couldn't do anything just because Farzana thought she'd seen something odd in Mike's file. But if Clemency were to see it for herself...

*

The next day was a Friday. Beirut airport was quiet, and the Red Air offices almost deserted. There were a couple of pilots in the crew room preparing their flight plan but they didn't give Clemency a second glance. The administrative office beyond was open, and she entered it as if she had every right to be there. Inside were two desks, one with a typewriter under a canvas cover, the other empty except for a telephone. This was where Rossiter worked when he was in Beirut. There were maps on the wall, cheaply-framed pictures of aircraft in flight, a sideboard where the drinks were locked away. Knowing the ways of pilots, that would have much stronger protection than the personnel files.

She stood for a moment, listening. Outside the terminal building, someone was performing a static test on an engine, bringing it up to full power. But she could still hear one of the pilots on the phone to the local met office, reading back the forecast to check there were no errors. She had to hope that she would also hear anyone approaching.

First off, she tackled the lock on the stationery cupboard. Anyone would understand her coming in to pinch a pencil or a notebook, and with luck would ask no more questions. It took her less than a minute to turn the lock over, and she opened it up. Some blue airmail envelopes and a pad of matching paper would be excuse enough. She left the cupboard open to catch the eye of anyone coming in while she turned to the first of the filing cabinets. The drawers were marked alphabetically, and again it didn't take long to flip open the lock. She winced as the drawer rattled as she pulled it open too quickly, but she doubted it could be heard in the crew room. In seconds, she had Mike's file open.

Nothing.

The file was empty. She checked again in the cabinet, but there was nothing in the space between *Tony Scott, Pilot*, and *Vanda Tanzetti, Stewardess*.

The file had the crease-marks to show it had once been filled with documents. But someone had removed every one.

She slid the file back into its place, and at once a

horrible thought came to her. Was this a trap? It would be so easy to have marked it with a slip of paper or a human hair to show if it had been taken out and examined.

She looked around her, as if expecting Rossiter himself to leap out from behind the battered sofa in the far corner. She drew a deep breath, reminding herself that Rossiter could hardly complain if she checked up on the crew. After all, she was there to keep his plane safe.

In any case, it would mean that Farzana had helped set the trap, and that certainly didn't fit.

She locked the cabinets again and let herself back into the corridor.

'Caroline!'

She spun round to find Bill Macquarie, amused to have caught her out.

'Stealing the paperclips?'

'Envelopes,' she replied, holding them up with a rueful grin.

'Anyway, a bit of luck, you being here. D'you want to go for a spin?'

Was Macquarie asking her out?

'Where to?'

'Zebra Victor is having its A check and I'm down to test her out. We do it out at sea, in case anything falls off. You might like to come for the ride.'

She joked about it not being the most enticing offer, but she was glad she had said yes because they had two hours putting the plane through its paces, and the flight engineer was happy for Clemency to sit in the co-pilot's seat, and Macquarie told her which levers to pull and switches to flick, and why. It reminded her of sitting in the organ loft of the church at home, watching

Miss Murphy practicing the hymns on Wednesday afternoons, awed by the array of knobs and pedals, the three – *three* – keyboards, and how Miss Murphy, so quiet and reserved, could control this monster and produce such spirited music.

She'd never been able to persuade her father to let her learn the organ herself, and so to play with this infinitely more powerful machine was deeply satisfying. Mr Kahn, the ground engineer, watched indulgently while keeping a close eye on the engine gauges; and Macquarie said very little. But when Kahn went to fetch coffee – and it really felt like a day off when she didn't have to do that – Macquarie tapped her on the shoulder.

'It's times like this… I remember why I became a pilot.'

'It's beautiful up here,' she replied. They were working their way down the coast from Sidon, and it seemed every few minutes there was another ruined Crusader castle, or a Roman temple, or a tiny fishing village around a sapphire-blue cove.

'I'm almost done,' he said, and it took her a moment to know what he meant.

'That's right,' he went on. 'I'm sixty-five next month. Time to hang up my cap.'

'What will you do?'

'I've no idea,' he replied. 'Maybe go back home. I grew up in a place called Hall's Creek in Western Australia. I haven't been there for years, but my sister's there and there's still people who'd know me. I suppose it's the closest I have to a home.'

'Do you have children?'

'I kind of missed out on all that. The years before the war weren't a good time for settling down, and then the war itself. But then again I've been lucky with nieces and nephews.'

He broke off to discuss something technical with the ground engineer and Clemency looked out over the Lebanese coast, bathed in the same afternoon light she had seen when she first arrived, all rose and sand, buff and russet, except for the blue of the swimming pools and the occasional diamond glint as the light bounced off a window.

There was a poem hovering on the edge of her mind, a relic of school, about a proud eagle gazing over the sea from its eyrie, and the co-pilot's seat was giving her the same sense of superiority. Those on the ground – even the rich businessmen and the film stars and the models sunning themselves beside the pools – they were like ants to her, crawling about, not feared or disliked but simply irrelevant.

No wonder pilots were so arrogant. No, that wasn't fair; not Macquarie anyway. He must have known how much she'd enjoy this jaunt.

'You OK if Miss Green here takes her in, Singit? She's done it before.'

The engineer didn't seem delighted by the idea, but the landing went smoothly. Macquarie insisted on her resting her hands on the control column in front of her and feeling how he handled the controls on the approach. There was no anxiety, just calmness and certainty in each movement, like a surgeon.

'Maybe one day you'll get the flying bug, Miss Green. Then you'll be a step ahead. After this ship, a Cessna or a Chipmunk will be a doddle.'

They returned to the crew mess just as Farzana was signing off from her return flight from Tehran.

'Is this not your day off?' she asked, and Clemency

had the odd feeling that Farzana knew why she was there.

'She was giving me a hand with Peter Zebra,' Macquarie explained. 'The A check.'

'You are very lucky. You could not have a better teacher.'

There was something odd in Farzana's voice. It was as if she saw Clemency as a fellow conspirator; or perhaps a rival.

# 13

The next week the Emir's grandson, Khalid, was flying home from his boarding school in England. Clemency was told to go and meet him at the arrival gate and escort him to the Red Air flight.

It felt like a day out of school, strolling over to the far end of the airport terminal to wait for the BOAC Comet from London. She had nothing to do but to stand at the empty gate, watching the skies and waiting for an update from the control tower. She even found she could gossip with the BOAC stewardesses with ease, no longer self-conscious or worried she would reveal herself as an imposter. Whatever else the future might hold, she could always work as cabin crew.

The plane arrived, the passengers began to straggle over the tarmac, and she recognised Khalid at once: a solemn child, a little short for his age, in a sports jacket with the robes and white headdress of Ahmar worn over the top, carrying a hold-all in one hand and a hockey stick in the other. He recognised her uniform as she approached him.

Suddenly she was on the edge of tears, seeing this child, who had been so far from home, travelling alone, and returning to the duties and responsibilities of the ruling family; worse, one in which the natural ties of family were so strained that it was so readily accepted that one or other of his uncles was planning to kill his grandfather.

'Your Excellency,' she said, not sure if this were the right form. 'I'm Clemency. I hope you had a good flight.'

'Very good, thank you.' His voice was very clear, his accent faultless. 'They had salmon. Not from a tin, either. The real thing.'

He chatted on while they waited for the ground crew to empty the hold of baggage. She asked him about where he went to school, and what lessons he liked the most. But he wanted to talk about what he would do when he was home in Ahmar; feeding his grandfather's hawks; hunting gazelle in the desert.

They set off towards Zebra Peter, sitting shimmering in the distance in a heat haze. He insisted on carrying his suitcase, and she ended up with his holdall and the hockey stick.

'It was my grandfather who first took me hunting. Now it is my Uncle Suleiman. Or my Uncle Abdullah. Except that he is often away,' he added, mystified why anyone would exchange Ahmar for the Cote d'Azur. 'My Uncle Suleiman believes that it is important for me to learn the ways of the desert, though it is Abdul, my grandfather's camel master, who teaches me the most.' He rattled on about his gun, a Remington .410; the half-promise of something more substantial for his next birthday, if the reports from his school were good; and then to being out in the desert at night, sitting round the fire, waiting for dawn.

'It sounds very different from when I've been out with our local shoot.'

'You hunt too? Is this usual for women?'

They stopped to let a fuel truck pass in front of them.

'Well, not unusual. To be honest, it's not really my

thing. But if the alternative is being stuck indoors all day...'

She had a vision of her own home; rain; long afternoons reading in her room. But it was nothing like the homesickness that Khalid was feeling.

'Why do you have to go to school in England? Is there nowhere nearer?'

'There are schools in Cairo, but since the time of Nassar that is not possible. And there is the American school in Beirut. But it is useful to learn about the English. They are the masters here.'

She stopped dead. 'Is that how you see it? See us?'

He smiled; it was both friendly and indulgent.

'Of course. Perhaps like my masters at school, you are helping us prepare for our future. I cannot say. I am only a child.'

With that, he began to climb the stairs to the door of the plane.

*

There was no meeting that evening, so David suggested they meet earlier for an aperitif on the terrace of the Hotel St Georges. By six, they were sipping their drinks and watching the sun dip to the edge of the Mediterranean, setting the distant banks of cloud alight.

'You've been mixing with Royalty, haven't you?' David said.

'How so?' She was feeling aloof and unapproachable in a Bacall kind of way.

'Prince Mohammed was on the flight last week.'

'Oh yes,' she said vaguely. Her attention was on the Dior cocktail dress that a tall woman at a nearby table was wearing. Was there a way to tell if it was an original, or one of the copies that they could run up for next to nothing in the shop off the Avenue de Plaisir?

'Did you speak to him?'

'Only to offer him coffee. It would look a bit odd if I started chatting him up.'

'You talked to Khalid today.'

'That's different. He can't be more than fourteen. And he was travelling on his own.'

'Any palace gossip?'

'Of course not. He's a child.'

Yet Khalid's upbringing made him as mature as many of the young men she knew in England, seemingly only interested in drinking, music or cars. Or rather, Khalid was capable of seeing the world as an adult. He had been childlike in his delight at being invited up to the cockpit, but the way he'd talked to her of the desert, or the way he'd seized on her having been hunting, asking her about it again later as if determined to understand what it might mean, and whether it was relevant to Ahmar's future.

Would he one day be the Emir? If none of his uncles had male children – no, that was wrong, it was more about who from the ruling family could count on the support of the *Shura*. When that time came, he would be that much older than any of his half-brothers, and maybe that would give him an edge. Perhaps in twenty years in the future, one of Abdullah, Suleiman or Mohammed would be the Emir, and in his declining years. It would be Khalid, then in his prime, who would be plotting to take his place.

'Hello?'

'Oh, I'm sorry, David. I was miles away.'

'I can see that. I was asking about Mohammed? Did he say why he was travelling? Where he was going?'

'No, but he was flying on to Damascus.'

'Really? How do you know?'

'I checked his bags through.'

'Why on earth didn't you tell us?'

The schoolmaster tone infuriated her.

'Why?' she hissed. 'How was I to know it mattered? You're the spy. My job is to serve cocktails and clean up the sick.'

'That's not fair. You're at the meetings. Why don't you say more?'

'Why don't you explain to me now? Why does it matter that he went to Damascus?'

'Because of the coup. The new government's very close to Moscow, and if you wanted a safe place to work on your conspiracy, Damascus is ideal. Worse, the Ba'athists are pan-Arab. They'd love to spark a revolution in one of the Gulf states. They might even provide some military back-up. Imagine if he called for Arab help against the British. The Syrians have a brigade of paratroops. They could be flown into Ahmar in a pre-planned coup.'

He glanced at his watch.

'We really need to let SIS in Damascus know about this. We may have been spending too much time worrying about Nasser and Egypt. Maybe it's a Syrian connection. Look, I think I'll go and talk to Farringdon and see what he thinks.'

David caught the eye of the waiter and asked for the bill. Clemency had no idea what to do. If David were right, she'd missed a crucial piece of intelligence. Was she deluding herself to think she was making a worthwhile contribution to the mission? But how could she do that if they treated her like a secretary. She was being set up to fail.

They came onto the street a few minutes later, David looking around for a taxi.

'Do you want to come?'

'There's no need, is there?'

'Well, some people would want to tell Farringdon themselves. Make sure they got the credit. This could be a breakthrough, you know.'

'You can tell him,' she said.

'Hey, don't feel bad,' David said, looking at her closely. 'We all let things slip by us. It's the reason we need to talk, exchange notes.' When this didn't seem to cheer her up much, he took her in his arms. 'Come on. No-one's going to be angry with you.'

She was torn between pulling away from him in frustration or taking the comfort that was on offer. She didn't move. But she couldn't look him in the eye.

'I'll square Farringdon and say to him I think we should give you a proper briefing on the political situation out here. We've got what goes on in Ahmar pretty well taped, and there's no substantial political discontent. If Mohammed – or any of them – want to make the coup look like anything other than a dynastic squabble, they'll need some outside support.'

He found his cab; she turned down the offer to drop her back at the Rookery. She thought the walk would do her good. All it did was give her a blister.

*

Felicity didn't leave it long before coming to her room to ask Clemency how her hot date had gone.

'Well, he was a bit dull. And he simply cannot dance,' she added, needing something to say and remembering her first dinner with David. 'Not even badly. Just not.'

'What a let-down. He looked like such a hunk.'

'Really? When did you see him?'

'In the cabin. Seat 11C. He's flown a few times with us. I think he's a lawyer or something. Anyway, naughty you, dating a passenger.'

'How did you know it was him?'

'I guessed. I saw you talking a couple of times on the last flight down there, and I thought you never see anyone else, so I just added it up. I was right, wasn't I?'

Clemency was sobered; if it was that easy for Felicity, why did she think the GRU or the Ahmar conspirators wouldn't find out? She closed her eyes in mortification.

'Remembering every minute? Was he a good kisser?'

'We definitely didn't go that far,' Clemency said, trying to get back into the mood.

'Silly you. You have to take what fun comes your way in this life. Anyway, at least you'll be less disapproving of me now.'

'I'm never that.'

'You're like a big sister, thinking I can't look after myself. That reminds me. Gemal's still asking if you'll meet his friend. He's very insistent. I'm seeing him again on Thursday. We could make up a foursome.'

'I don't know…'

In fact, Clemency did know. She had no intention of going to a nightclub and meeting Gemal's friend, who would be generous to her with champagne and flattery and expect her to be equally generous in return.

'It'll be fun,' Felicity insisted. 'I told Gemal all about you and his friend is really keen to meet you. Oh, come on. Don't be a wet blanket. Gemal says his friend knows something about Red Air and I don't want to miss out if there's gossip going.'

'It's all right for you,' Clemency said. 'I'm flying the next day.'

But now she would go. Anyone asking about Red Air, or claiming to know something about it, had to be followed up.

'So drink mineral water,' Felicity said impatiently. 'Leave the champagne for me.'

Clemency pretended to waver, then gave in.

'All right, then. But home at midnight.'

'We'll see,' Felicity said, jumping up to return to her own room. 'You're not my fairy godmother, you know,' she called over her shoulder.

# 14

Since the day she arrived in Beirut, Clemency hadn't given much thought to Alec Rossiter. But the following morning, everyone she saw at the airport told her that the Boss wanted to see her, straight away, and making clear with different amounts of sympathy or glee that he was furious and that she was definitely for the high jump. It was hard to remember that she wasn't an employee, and that he couldn't actually fire her, and that in any case this wasn't her job.

There wasn't a lot of time before she was due on Peter Zebra, and lots of running around until she found him in one of the hangars with a group of men in oil-stained boiler suits, staring at an engine with its cowling off.

'Ah, Caroline. We're in trouble.' He gestured to her to follow him, talking as he went. 'You should have told the Lebanese protocol office about Khalid. They wanted to welcome him with all due respect.'

'But I checked. Grandsons of rulers don't count. Surely the son of a daughter counts for even less.'

'Very good. You're learning something about this part of the world. Even so, they've asked us to let them know when he returns.'

They reached the end of the hangar, far from the maintenance crew. In a lower voice, he asked her how the mission was going, and whether there was anything he could do to help. She was reassuring but non-committal, suggesting he ought to ask Farringdon or Vaughn.

'D'you think they're any good?' he asked bluntly.

'Oh yes,' she said loyally.

'Only they seem to think this is all about keeping the plane secure. I don't think that's right. We can keep Peter Zebra as tight as a mouse's arsehole and there's still no guarantees. For a few days, fine. Then people get slack. Six weeks is too long. A plane is just too vulnerable. Too many parts to sabotage or places to hide something.'

'What do you suggest?'

'Look, I just run a bloody airline. What do I know? But surely this is about proper intelligence work. Sussing out who's behind this plot and warning them off.'

She began to reassure him, but he cut across her, complaining that neither Vaughn nor Farringdon was making time to talk to him. Somehow he'd learned that Farringdon had been in Beirut and that had riled him.

'And the cheeky bugger flew out here on BOAC.'

He sounded off for a little longer, then switched to being more conciliatory.

'None of this is about you, by the way. I'm very pleased with how you're keeping what you're doing discreet. I've no complaints about your work, either. Talking of which, you'd better run along. Peter Zebra will be loading in ten minutes.'

She turned to go, but he grabbed her arm.

'But tell those buggers to talk to me. Right? Tell them I may know something useful about Mohammed.'

'Do you?'

'Of course not. But they don't know that, do they.' He grinned hugely, and for the first time she warmed to him a bit, the way he thought nothing of manipulating senior officers in MI5 and SIS.

'And like I said, anything that looks odd – anything at all – you come to me first. No blabbing to your colleagues.'

'Of course. Like the fruit.'

'Fruit? What fruit?'

She blushed.

'I thought you knew. About Mr Stannard.' She stammered out an explanation, with Rossiter looking more and more furious. But when she'd finished, or trailed off, he waved it away.

'Forget it. I don't mind a bit of free carriage for my pilots. But whatever you do, don't tell your people. Stannard's a damn good pilot and I don't want him getting into trouble. And by the way, if you want to fit in, go out with the other stews. Felicity was telling me how you don't join in. That makes you stand out. Go to a night club with her, or something. Just a friendly tip. Now off you go.'

She set off briskly across the hangar, but he shouted after her:

'Hey! Remember you've got a plane to get ready. Don't walk, run!'

*

Rossiter's complaint was an excuse to call Denholm when she got back from Baghdad. He suggested they meet for supper and she poured out Rossiter's frustrations and her own doubts.

'He's right about the plane being vulnerable. I feel like we're relying too much on our last line of defence. There's not really that much that David or I can do, is there? Not if they plant a bomb or get on board with guns.'

'Maybe not,' Denholm conceded.

'I keep hearing about all the intelligence work in Ahmar, but what exactly are they doing?'

'I don't know. I can guess, though. There's a standard way of doing these things. Tapping the phones, paid informers, trailing suspects to see where they go and who they meet, and then following them too. Then sifting everything you get back to try and build up some kind of picture.'

'But they're still talking about how it could be either Abdullah or Suleiman, when surely it's obvious that it must be Mohammed.'

'Well, you say that…'

'Mohammed is the only one who could be in league with the Communists, isn't he? The Cairo connection, and the trips to Damascus and Baghdad. The Soviets are hardly likely to be working to put either of the others on the throne.'

'There's such a thing as keeping an open mind.'

She pulled a face.

'Think of Abdullah,' he said. 'Maybe he would do anything, get into bed with anyone, if that's what it took to secure his birth-right.'

'Perhaps…'

'He may be lazy, but even lazy people can lash out if they're pushed far enough. Even Suleiman can't be ruled out. His brand of fundamentalism might seem like a medieval relic, but it gains power from its very purity.'

Perhaps seeing the doubt on her face, Denholm plunged on.

'Nationalism is a powerful force. But the Arab

nationalists have a problem. They want to reject the West, but they also want to build – or claim to want to build – a Western society, with democracy and tolerance and all the compromises and complexity and frustrations that democracy must bring. That makes them vulnerable to being outflanked by something more extreme. The religious nationalists, as you might call them, have something more potent to offer the masses. Expelling the foreigners and their ideas. Returning to the glory days of the Caliphates. Turning violence into a religious act.'

'But the Soviets would never back it.'

'Wouldn't they? They might not worry about the long-term consequences if there's a short-term advantage to be gained. Or they might think that, once he's made his move, they can push him to one side. I'm not saying you're wrong to say it's most probably Mohammed. Only you need to…'

'Stick to my job?'

She felt bad about needling him; but it was because he listened and took her seriously. The others would have treated her like a child, with false reassurances.

'You're a volunteer, Clemency. You can always stop.'

'Can I?' She tried to smile. 'I think it's far too late for that.'

*

The next day, Stannard stopped in the galley as he came on board.

'Do you have the passenger list?' he asked abruptly. Surprised, she passed it to him. He scanned it and looked up at her, frowning.

'Who is this chap in 11C?'

She made a show of taking the list back and consulting it.

'Mr Fletcher. He's one of our regulars.'

This didn't seem to reassure Stannard; quite the opposite.

'Yes, but who is he? Why is he on the same flight every week?'

It was tempting to tell Stannard to ask him himself, but she bit her tongue instead.

'Is he the one who's always chatting to you?'

'No more than the other passengers.'

'Look, Caroline, I don't get too much involved with the cabin crew side of things. I leave that to the senior stewardess. But when it comes to one of the crew making a fool of herself— '

'That's not fair!'

'—and letting down the side, then I'm entitled to say something. If necessary, to Rossiter. Get you moved. It reflects on the professionalism of the crew and the airline.'

'Has anyone complained?'

'No, but who is he? Why does he keep coming on the flight?'

'He works at the Residency in Ahmar and he has to come up to Beirut each week for some kind of meeting or other. That's all I know. I think he might be an accountant. He said he's only here for a few weeks.'

'Is he? And thinks he can play around with our stewardesses before he goes back to marital bliss in Bromley or wherever. Well, you've got to burn him off. Get him seated away from the galley for one thing.'

'I don't book the seats.'

'For God's sake, Caroline, use your initiative. Talk to the check-in clerk at Ahmar. Get him to do it. And find out anything else you can about him. I don't think it sounds right. Any of it.'

He banged out of the galley and clattered down the stairs onto the tarmac. Caroline closed her eyes and sighed. Her hands were shaking and she wanted to lock herself away somewhere, though whether to laugh or cry she couldn't be sure. The whole thing was farcical – two men locking horns over her, and she having no interest – none at all – in either of them. But it was dangerous. If Stannard kept digging, it could expose David's role. If he were in the same seat – and she was coming to hate 11C – on the next flight, Stannard would blow a fuse. But if David had to move, he couldn't do his job so well.

She went to sit down and found Felicity in the cabin quietly folding blankets. She smirked at Clemency.

'Well…'

'There's nothing to it,' she protested. 'Mike must have been out in the sun and he's imagining things.'

'Sounded like he was proposing. Quite Victorian, really. *Are 11C's intentions honourable?*' she mimicked. '*I alone love you, Caroline. We will be wed on the morrow.* Can I be a bridesmaid?'

'I'm not in the mood.'

'Where will you live? How many children will you have? What will you call them?'

'What am I going to do?'

'Stop stringing 11C along,' Felicity said decidedly. 'Let him take you out for dinner again. Then you can decide what you want to do with him. If he's not your type, then get him moved somewhere else in the cabin.

It doesn't matter if he's upset. If he is your type, fine, you can still move him because he gets to see you in the evenings.'

Felicity's logic was impeccable. Clemency felt all the more trapped.

# 15

Everything about the Wednesday flight was normal until Clemency took the pilots their lunches. Stannard, who usually demolished whatever was put in front of him, waved the tray away and asked for more black coffee.

'The greedy bugger ate too much last night,' Macquarie said without sympathy. 'Now he's paying for it.'

Stannard just looked miserable.

The guinea fowl had a better reception in the main cabin. Abdullah, returning with his father and seated in the row behind with an American businessman, was in particularly good spirits. Unusually, he thanked her when she took away his tray.

'Is there anything else you would like, Your Highness?'

He turned to his companion.

'I am sure some of that excellent brandy would be welcome. I suspect the ever-present fear of a fiery death gives it extra piquancy. Oh, don't look so shocked, my dear. I am in jest. I am sure this fine sturdy aeroplane will arrive safely.'

Clemency managed a smile.

'And perhaps some coffee?'

He shuddered. 'Mint tea,' he said decidedly.

As she poured the brandy and unpacked the special glass and fresh mint leaves for Abdullah, she wondered if there were some hidden meaning behind his words. It couldn't be a warning. If he knew something definite, he'd have been demanding that the plane land, not enjoying honey-glazed guinea fowl with almonds and pomegranate. Or was he gloating inside, knowing that on their next flight she and the other passengers would indeed be blown from the sky, while he was safely playing the tables at Monaco?

She carried the drinks to the front of the plane, placing them with as much ceremony as she could manage as they ran through a patch of mild turbulence.

'Do take the utmost care,' Abdullah said. 'It would not do to spill alcohol on me.'

She guessed he was joking, despite the straight face.

'You ever touch the stuff?' his companion asked.

'Never. But I try to place myself next to all temptations. Fine wines, aged brandies, beautiful girls...' He gestured to Clemency. 'In this way, my observance of the Law is all the more worthy.'

Soon it was time for the set-down into Ahmar and Clemency rapped on the door of the toilet to warn the occupant. There was no reply, only a feeble groan. Farzana touched her shoulder.

'The Captain is asking for you.'

Clemency went to the cockpit, where Macquarie was in a particularly jovial mood.

'I should set up as a bloody fortune teller. One week I teach my stewardess to fly, the next I lose my co-pilot.'

It took Clemency a moment to work out he wasn't joking.

'Where's Mr Stannard.'

'In the dunny. Likely to stay there, I fear. So if you

have nothing better to do, could you help me get this ship down on the ground?'

There were a hundred reasons to protest or questions to ask; but his calm assumption that she would help silenced them. Instead she climbed into the seat and strapped herself in.

'What do I do?'

'Remind yourself of the controls. I'll take the throttles, you take the flaps. Call out if the airspeed goes below 120. Which one is the flaps?'

'This wheel here?'

'Good girl.'

Macquarie ran her through the controls and settings again and again, and all the time the airstrip was coming closer, the height falling away.

'I've always said that cabin crew should learn the basics of flight so they can help out. You should see the figures for the number of pilots who collapse in the air.'

He seemed delighted. She just wanted it to be over. They were coming over the sea, and from the vantage-point of the cockpit it looked much too close.

'Flaps thirty.'

'Flaps thirty,' she repeated as she turned the wheel, just as he'd told her to.

'Speed?'

'130.'

He began to hum a tune as they lined up on the runway, the lights surprisingly clear even under the midday sun. She glanced at the airspeed, still steady at 130, and they continued their strangely slow approach, like a ferry coming into dock, giving the impression there was plenty of time, but knowing that a mistake could quickly turn this calm into disaster.

She found her hands gripping the steel frame of her seat.

'You'll need to watch out when we get back to Beirut,' Macquarie said conversationally. 'The Boss is on the warpath about the duty-free sales. Says you girls aren't pushing hard enough.'

'Thanks for the tip,' she replied. '125.'

They slipped from sea to land and over the fence that marked the edge of the aerodrome. Macquarie eased the nose up a little, rolled back the throttles and the plane settled gently onto the runway. He reversed the engines and soon they were slowing, and Clemency could let out her breath. Clearly, he could have landed the plane safely on his own; but she was still proud to have helped.

He looked over at her and winked, then picked up the microphone and made the usual announcement welcoming the passengers to Ahmar; except that it was on behalf of First Officer Green and the crew. He didn't look at her, but his weather-beaten face was lit up with mischief. She just hoped Stannard hadn't heard.

Once they'd helped Stannard over to the terminal and called a doctor, Macquarie told the Red Air clerk to start calling the passengers and telling them that the return flight was delayed until the morning.

'We can't take off with just one pilot,' he said. 'If anything happened to me, we'd be right up the creek. I reckon Mike'll be OK tomorrow. You get these 24-hour bugs.'

They readied the plane for an early start and then drove over to the old fort, now a government guest house. From behind the canvas hood of the Land-Rover, Clemency had an impression of vast sandstone walls, tiny windows protected with wooden shutters bleached by years of sun, and then they were inside and being shown to their rooms.

Perhaps she should have tried to find David or explore the town. What she actually did was have a cold shower – in fact, the water was blood-hot – and then go to sleep in the plain, shuttered room at the top of one of the towers. When she woke, it was nearly dark and there was an invitation waiting for Macquarie and her to dine at the mess at the Residency. Macquarie would be all right in his uniform, but Clemency knew she'd feel horribly out of place in hers; she'd have to hope that, like shipwrecked mariners, they would be given some licence. It was still daunting to arrive at the Residency, a long, low white building in the colonial style, shaded by palms and with lawns to either side, and a servant in a tarboosh stood waiting at the top of the stairs.

'Bet you wished you'd packed your tiara,' Macquarie whispered to her. 'They live like royalty, don't they?'

Then David appeared, and at once she felt more relaxed, and wasn't even too anxious when he led them into the drawing room to meet the Resident. She had expected Lawrence of Arabia – maybe not the robes, but certainly tall, lean, perhaps the steely glare of a bird of prey. Sir Reginald Calthrop was more like a bank manager; nothing legendary or heroic, and hard to see him crossing the Empty Quarter on a camel or hunting gazelle with the Emir. But when she hinted at this quietly to David over the soup, he was merely amused.

'That's all way in the past,' he said. 'It's all economics and diplomacy now.'

As if aware that he was the subject of her interest, Sir Reginald chose that moment to look across the table to her.

'And what does your father do, Miss Green?'

'He's a surgeon.'

'Is he?' There was a tinge of surprise in Calthrop's voice, and Clemency could feel herself being lifted a few notches up the social scale.

'My mother was a nurse, until they married.'

'Well, then you're keeping up a family tradition. The first air stewardesses on Imperial Airways were former nurses.'

Clemency was used to being told things that she already knew. She just smiled.

'I've been very well looked-after by Miss Green and her colleagues on my weekly flights,' David said. 'Tonight is by way of a thank you.'

'We've got to thank you, Mr Fleming,' Macquarie said, 'I'm not grumbling, but the Fort's a bit basic. We'd have been dining on tinned soup, crackers and Gentleman's Relish.'

'I doubt you'd have found that in Ahmar, Captain Macquarie,' Calthorp said dryly.

'We carry it in the hold, sir. It's quite a little delicatessen down there. Six bottles of Worcestershire Sauce, twenty-four cans of luncheon meat, the same of corned beef, forty-eight packets of crackers. Soup, biscuits, tea and coffee, tinned milk and chocolate. If we ever had to put down in the desert we'd be all right for a couple of days at least, even with a full complement of passengers.'

'Choose a day when I'm not on board, eh?' David said.

'How do you find the people up at the airfield?'

the Resident said. 'The Arab workers? How reliable are they?'

'Well, all the technical work is done back at Beirut,' Macquarie explained. 'All they're doing is loading and unloading, plus the fuel. There's an agent at the field, an Iraqi, who manages all of that.'

The Resident seemed pleased to hear it; Clemency saw that this wasn't just small talk, and that the Resident really was trying to gain some insight into the country that in effect he ruled jointly with the Emir. It was bizarre; but all of a part of the way he and his staff lived apart. Instead of dining with the Ahmaris, they ate in this stuffy isolation each night.

Then she realised why Farzana had said she had a headache; she would not have been welcome here. Like the Iraqi airfield manager, or the Maltese clerks in the Residency, she was too near to being a native. What hurt most was that Clemency hadn't understood; had been rattling on to Farzana about how kind it was that she'd volunteered to stay with Stannard, although he was making a good recovery. She felt so stupid.

The meal wound on; her spirits sank further. Every observation made seemed to be the obvious one; every topic of conversation entirely predictable. This was the nerve centre of the British Protectorate, and yet they were so dull. The few dinner parties at her parents' home that she'd been unable to avoid had been far more entertaining than this; even gossip about surgeons in a district hospital had more colour and meaning.

'We don't normally worry about leaving the gentlemen to their port,' Lady Margaret said to Clemency. 'It would be rather hard on me, I feel,' she added with a little laugh. 'We usually take coffee in the garden.'

'I was wondering if Miss Green might like to have a look at the walls,' David said smoothly. 'They are most impressive.'

The Resident looked a bit put out; exchanged a glance with Lady Margaret; then he must have remembered what David and Clemency were there for, because his brow cleared.

'What a good idea,' he said. 'They are jolly romantic in the moonlight.'

It was an unfortunate choice of words; Lady Margaret clearly thought the young people were letting the side down. But it was at least a chance of escape.

David helped her into her *abaya* and they set off down the track to the town walls.

'What an evening!' she said as soon as it felt safe to speak. 'I thought I'd scream.'

'They're not so bad, the Residency crowd, once you get to know them.'

'It was painful. Victorian.'

'Don't be prejudiced by the Empire manner. He's got a shrewd head on his shoulders. Lady Margaret too, for that matter.'

Clemency let it slide. There were few enough chances to talk about the mission. But whatever David wanted to say, he was biding his time. They walked on in silence, and Clemency became aware of the night around them, still and quiet. Their feet made no sound on the sandy path. From far away, in the town, a dog barked.

'Are we safe here?' she asked, looking at the grove of palms to their left.

'There's never any trouble in Ahmar.'

'If that were true, we could go home tomorrow.'

They came to the walls. The path went in through a gateway, no more than an inky pool of shadow. But

David took her hand to guide her to the foot of the steps that led up to the battlements.

They emerged into moonlight and could look out over the desert to one side and the jumble of roofs to the other. There were voices coming from a room nearby; women's voices, speaking in Arabic; then a burst of laughter.

'What's going on?' Clemency asked. 'Have you learned something new?'

'What? Oh, no. Same old story. Lots of rumours and nothing concrete.'

'I'm not surprised, if they lock themselves away in the Residency like that. They should be out talking to people.'

'D'you know, you might be right. I imagine it must be a bit like this if you're in the police in the East End of London. No-one will talk. It's like a secret society. They're very polite and sometimes seem quite open but actually they are weighing every word.'

'Do you think we're any closer to finding out who's behind it?'

He looked pained.

'A little. I think Abdullah is in the clear. But the other two – the hangers-on around them keep hinting that the other man can't be trusted, but when you try and pin them down to specifics…'

'And the Soviets?'

'Sir Reginald's convinced that the Gulf Arabs will never take the Communists seriously. It's still feudal here. There's no urban middle class, no factory workers, no disaffected students or intelligentsia, no unions. Of course, he's right – but that doesn't mean one or other of them wouldn't take help from Nasser or the Soviets if it were offered. Or weapons, for that matter.'

It was reassuring to Clemency that, away from the Residency, David was more of his own man.

'I think you're right to keep the Soviets in mind. Are there many Egyptians working here? Or Palestinians?'

'You have been doing your homework,' he said. 'And is it right you're learning Arabic?'

'*Faqat kalimat qalila.* One of the ground staff at Beirut is helping me.'

He turned to her, his smile showing white in the darkness.

'You really are full of surprises, Clemency.'

She sensed a shift in his mood.

'I just hate being left out of any conversation,' she said lightly.

'No, I mean it. When they said that I'd be working with a girl, I thought it was a bit of a joke. When I found out you were going to be a stewardess, then it just seemed irrelevant. But I feel we're partners now. Don't you?'

'Yes… yes, I do.'

'The only problem is that I also assumed you'd be an ex-policewoman with a face like the back end of a bus. But instead…'

He stopped and leaned over the wall.

'I don't get how you stay so calm on the plane,' he said casually. 'I watch you walking up and down, smiling and keeping everyone happy. Yet all the time you know what the risk is. Me, I'm on the edge all the time. Sometimes I think I'd like there to be a hijack so I'd have something to do. Or because a hijack is better than a bomb.'

'Don't say that.'

'It's true. Don't you think of that every time we're climbing after we leave the airport? Any minute now and the bomb will go off? Will it be now? Or now? Or maybe now? No, I bet you don't. You have nerves of ice.'

'You don't know me very well if you think that.'

'Do you worry too?' It suddenly seemed very important to him. 'Scared? I thought it was just me. If it were a man with a gun, I'd be on him like a terrier. It's the... the way you just have to wait for the axe to fall. They used to say that the worst job during the war was being on a merchant ship. You plod along at sea waiting for the torpedo, no way to fight back, nothing to do for days or weeks on end. It gets on your nerves. That's how I feel, anyway.

'And the other thing... I think to myself, when this is over, I'll ask Clemency out. Then I think, there's someone else, isn't there? Sorry, I shouldn't ask you.'

'It's OK. But yes, there is.'

'It's a shame,' he said. 'Look at all this.'

He gestured towards the palm trees; the creek silvered in the moonlight, lined with moored dhows; the mysterious depths of the town; the elegant lance of the minaret. It was quite beautiful.

'I'm not very good at chatting girls up, and the whole moon and June thing. But with this behind me, how could I fail?'

'If there wasn't someone else, then maybe you wouldn't need any of this.'

It was what he wanted, needed, to hear; and yet it wasn't entirely untrue. She too wanted the comfort of feeling that someone cared. At some point he'd taken her hand. Was she being disloyal to Peter? It didn't feel that way. They were all on the same side, and feeling sorry for David didn't make what she felt for Peter any the less.

‘I should go.’

‘Yes.’

Neither moved. It took the screech of a cat in the alley below them to break the spell.

# 16

Clemency insisted on walking back to the Fort on her own. It was a chance to clear her mind. How could she have let David hold her hand like that? She hadn't encouraged him, but she hadn't drawn back either. But how could she have pushed him away? He was far more on edge, far more distressed by the strain of the mission, than she would ever have expected. If he wanted to flirt, and it boosted his ego, or distracted him from his fears, then it was her duty to go along. But it was still ridiculous; the only reason she was here was because of Peter.

She plodded on, thinking instead of Sir Reginald. She'd expected Her Majesty's Resident Advisor to have a deep knowledge of the Arab people, and a web of contacts stretching to every oasis, every camel train and dhow. Instead, he and his aides insisted on holding themselves apart from the people they were supposed to be serving. Even Farzana was not welcome at their table.

At last she reached the Fort. Apart from the doorman, who emerged from a little cubicle to let her in, everything was quiet, the public rooms deserted. She went up to Farzana's room, hoping to have the chance to apologise for leaving her alone. But it was empty.

Next she went to Mike Stannard's room, but she wasn't there. Nor was Mike.

There were any number of explanations, but one underlying feeling; that something odd was going on.

Then she thought of the plane, standing out on the airstrip.

Should she go back to the Residency and find David? That would take an hour or more. Or wait for Macquarie to return? Any explanations must reveal her identity. Better to go and see for herself.

The moon was lower in the sky now but there was still more than enough light for her to follow the track to the airstrip. Soon she could see the familiar outline of Zebra Peter, black against the starlight. Everything was still and silent. She walked cautiously forward, wondering what was missing, until she realised that there were no guards.

The airstairs were in place and the rear door stood open. She imagined she saw some movement inside, but it was gone before she could be sure. Even so, nothing on earth would have induced her to go inside, alone and unarmed. She slunk into the cover of the undercarriage, wrapped her *abaya* around her, and settled down to wait.

A few minutes passed. Then came a faint scrape of metal from the front of the plane: the emergency hatch in the cockpit. A moment later, she was on her feet and running silently along the line of the fuselage. A dark figure dropped to the ground right in front of her. Clemency lunged, scrabbling for a hold, kicked in the side but hanging on as the other cursed. The voice, the almond scent of her hair; Clemency stopped struggling.

'Farzana?'

*

Farzana's explanation was simple enough. She had suddenly realised that the plane had been left unlocked, unguarded, and that thieves could get on board and strip it bare. She'd come to secure it and was checking that nothing had been taken when she heard a stealthy sound by the rear exit. After a time of standing frozen with fear inside the plane, she'd remembered the exit from the cockpit.

Clemency said she'd thought much the same, and in their mutual relief it was easy to find the whole thing a joke.

Even Stannard's vanishing had a simple explanation; he'd told Farzana that he felt a lot better and that a walk would do him good and that he didn't need any more cosseting, as he put it.

Farzana suggested checking the plane over in case anything had been stolen, which was ideal for Clemency to see if anything had been left hidden, or there were any traces of sabotage. It took a long time, and once they had finished there wasn't an obvious way to secure the plane, and so they ended up staying there for what was left of the night, each wrapped in half a dozen of the small airline blankets against the cold.

Farzana had made tea and as they drank it, she talked about her family, the village where she grew up, about the horses she'd had as a child and riding up into the mountains in the spring when the snows retreated and the rocky soil bloomed with flowers. And she was just as interested in hearing about Clemency's life, and particularly her parent's home, delighting her that it was not so very different from the world she knew from the novels of Jane Austen.

It was all a bit like being at school or guide's camp, with Farzana as her new best friend. But part of her mind baulked at the coincidence. Could Farzana be working for one of the Emir's sons? Was she on the plane for some sinister purpose? Not a bomb, surely, because she too would die with the rest of them. But she might smuggle on board the guns needed for a hijacking. Anything was possible. Perhaps beneath the calm, friendly façade, Farzana was a committed Communist.

And Stannard? The tale of a night stroll to settle his stomach was even more bizarre than finding Farzana sneaking around the plane. Was the whole illness faked? Perhaps to delay the flight and leave the plane vulnerable?

The more she thought of it, the more it fitted. Stannard made a much better villain than Farzana, dozing contently in her blankets.

*

Clemency got some sleep herself in the end, but it seemed like no time before Macquarie appeared in the grey light of the dawn. He was annoyed because Stannard, despite all the trouble of the day before, had gone off to the souk to fetch his crates of fruit, leaving Macquarie to do the pre-flight checks. He took his temper out on Clemency and Farzana.

'Come on, you two. No time for floating about. I want to be in the air by seven.'

'I'll make him some breakfast,' Farzana whispered. 'You start checking in the passengers.'

'And by the way, you both look bloody awful. Did you go on to a nightclub?' he added, with a hint of returning good humour.

The passengers were already assembling in the

terminal building, eager to be off, or at least to get on board where there would be coffee or something stronger. She checked them in until David presented himself at the counter.

'Oh, Mr Fletcher. I'm afraid we'll need to reconfirm your ticket. Could you come with me?'

She led him into an empty office.

'There's really no need to apologise about last night,' he said with a smile. 'Water under the bridge.'

She was already angry, so this passed her by.

'There was no guard on the plane last night.'

He looked puzzled; then concerned.

'Are you sure?'

'I checked, after I left you. Anyone could have got on board.'

He didn't need to know about the pantomime with Farzana and the empty plane.

'Major Hereward is away at the moment,' he said defensively. 'I don't expect he left orders about guarding the plane if it was here overnight. What are we going to do? Can we check it over?'

'I think it's OK. I had a look around and then I slept on the plane.'

'Yes, you do look a bit bedraggled. Anyway, on that basis I say we carry on with the flight. After all, another day sitting out here while they take the plane to pieces to look for sabotage or a bomb is going to be hard to keep under wraps.'

For once, she was glad it wasn't her decision. On the one hand, the forty lives on the plane; on the other, the risk of blowing the whole operation. Perhaps she was being unfair about the night before. He was under stress too; perhaps all the more so for being in charge and having these kinds of calls to make.

'And David, I am sorry. Even if it doesn't need saying.'

'Hey, don't worry. We'll pick it up another time.'

*

Suleiman was on the flight. He could not have been more of a contrast to his brother Abdullah. He was thin, his beard was long and untrimmed, and he never smiled. He was travelling with a cleric, Ayman Al-Salaam, but they parted at the door of the plane. Suleiman went forward to sit with his father, making a great show of deference, leaving Clemency to show Al-Salaam to his seat. He had the venomous air of a man who feared and hated flying and resented all those who worked for the airlines. Once they were airborne, he waved away any offers of food impatiently, except demanding that his glass of iced water be refilled regularly.

'Have I done something wrong?' she whispered to Farzana as they passed in the galley.

'Him? No. He hates us all. We do not wear the veil and we work outside the home. Therefore, we are followers of Satan.'

'Is Prince Suleiman the same? His brothers aren't like that.'

'Exactly.'

As Clemency served the main course, she thought of Suleiman growing up in the palace as the youngest son, desperate to win the approval of his father. With Abdullah given over to self-indulgence and Mohammed seeking to smash every tradition, what better way than to gain attention than by taking the Emir's respect for the religious and pursuing it to an extreme?

Just then the plane ran into some turbulence and

Clemency had to grab a seat back to stop herself from falling. She managed to serve the rest of the meals, then fetched the jug of water for Al-Salaam. Typically, the plane lurched again at the wrong moment and water splashed onto his robes. Even so, she was startled by the look of hatred he shot at her.

Then she noticed the engine noise. The pitch had risen a few notes, and there was a little extra weight as the plane began to climb. Suppressing her fear, she went back to the galley and began to secure anything loose.

Then the light went on to summon her to the flight deck.

'Better get them all belted up,' Macquarie said. 'We're running into a storm and I don't think we can go round or climb over. And Caroline,' he added, turning to her. 'It might be a bad'un.'

It felt bad enough already as she returned to the cabin. Farzana was taking the trays back from reluctant passengers and asking them to fasten their belts. Then the plane seemed to drop into a hole and food and drink went everywhere. She started in on collecting what she could and mopping people down. The Emir was calm, but his daughter Fatima looked anxious and his secretary was gripping the arms of his seat and praying.

Once her hands were full, Clemency half-ran to the galley and began slotting the trays back into the storage compartments.

'No time for that,' Farzana snapped. 'Look.'

Outside the sky had turned almost black, the towering clouds made all the more ominous by the remnants of the sunlight that lit their edges. There were flashes of lightning.

Clemency helped fetch the last few glasses. As she

passed David, she saw he was looking sickly, his skin greenish and sweaty. He grabbed her arm as she passed.

'What's going on? We've got to turn back!'

'We'll be fine,' she said, as if to a frightened child. 'I've spoken to the Captain. The plane is perfectly safe.'

She used the same formula on two other passengers – both large, capable men who looked like they could deal with any emergency, from a well-head fire to armed bandits, so long as their feet were fixed to the earth.

With the trays cleared, she ran down the aisle to report to Farzana, only to find herself floating as the plane dipped, then about to stumble as it rose beneath her. She held her nose, the only way to stop herself from being sick.

Ignoring her, Farzana made an announcement.

'Ladies and gentlemen, the Captain has asked that you remain in your seats until the weather improves. Please be assured that there is no danger. But the flight will be uncomfortable. Please do not undo your belt or leave your seat for any reason. If you feel unwell you will find a bag in the pocket of the seat in front of you. If—'

Then Clemency was falling upwards. The ceiling slammed into her and she stayed pinned there, looking down on the astonished faces of the Emir and his party. The engines screamed and the cabin was filled with papers, blankets, clothing, vomit. Then, just as she realised how much it was going to hurt, the plane rose again and she was flung to the floor. She felt like lead, the blood draining away, her head spinning, and then she was released. Farzana helped her to the jump seats and they buckled themselves in.

The engines had spooled back to idle, and it was eerily quiet; and then another crash as the plane seemed to want to come to pieces. After that it was a nightmare of a fairground ride which never seemed to end; switchback after switchback, then an agonising pause on the edge of a plunge, a twist to one side as the storm tried to flip the plane over. She tried to imagine what it must be like in the cockpit; but maybe for them this was bearable because they could at least do something; not sit strapped in, helpless and afraid.

Her one aim was to avoid the humiliation of being sick, and it helped that she hadn't eaten for hours. She was also glad to be sitting opposite the Emir, who simply closed his eyes and composed himself to endure; and his daughter, who was observing Clemency and Farzana as if they were the subject of a medical experiment. Across the aisle, Suleiman was making a show of calm, not looking up from the book he was reading, as if he had no interest in the storm, or placed his faith in Allah.

Then, as quickly as it had come on, they were flying straight and level once again. Farzana slipped from her seat and into the cockpit. When she returned, she whispered in Clemency's ear.

'This is the bad bit.' She handed Clemency a plastic sack and a wad of cloths. 'The first aid kit is just up here if anyone's hurt.'

They began to work their way down the aisle, helping the passengers to clean themselves up. Each was dealing with their experience in their own way; one a seasoned traveller, who wanted to show they'd never been afraid; another embarrassed to have to hand, mutely, a bag of sick to her; another still shaking but already turning to anger, demanding to know what the pilot was thinking of, why they had not avoided the storm, why the stewardesses had not come when he had summoned them for assistance.

But the worst was David. He managed a smile, but his eyes betrayed him. He was ashamed that he'd been so frightened; and that she had seen him in this state.

'Quite a ride,' he said. 'Are you all right?'

'Just bruised.'

'I thought you'd had it when we dropped like that. Well, I thought we all had, to be honest.'

'Nothing that a hot bath won't fix. I'm on duty tomorrow morning at six.'

'You're going to carry on? Like nothing happened?'

There was something about his manner that irritated her. There was no point in him acting chivalric. If the plane hit rough weather, there was nothing he could do to protect her.

'I have to,' she snapped. 'It's my job. Yours too.'

'Yes.' His gaze turned inward. 'Yes, I suppose it is.'

# 17

After the flight, they left Stannard to fuss over his cargo, spilled all over the hold, and went down to the Club. There was a cool breeze coming in from the sea. She swam for a while, then sat on one of the loungers with a *citron pressé*, not wanting to start on alcohol when there was the weekly meeting to attend.

Felicity was saying she felt like a change of scene, and that she might put in for a job with another airline, perhaps in the Far East. Macquarie was passing on some cautionary tales, based on his service with Cathay Pacific many years before. Clemency let her mind drift, watching a young couple in the pool, fair and tanned. They were both excellent swimmers, and were playing at pulling each other underwater, then coming up for air and protesting and starting all over again. Watching enviously, she thought of Peter. What if he never came back? Was she going to live her whole life waiting for him? But if not, how long was enough? And what would he do, if she had been the one dragged off by Petrov? You could say it was different for a man, but…

The couple – German, perhaps – were racing each other up and down, and he was teasing her by letting her almost win, and then nosing ahead at the end. Then they kissed, and decided to leave the pool, and settled themselves near to Clemency.

'Please excuse me,' the girl said. 'But might you take a picture? Of us?'

'Of course.'

They showed Clemency how the camera worked – a German make she'd never seen before – and they arranged themselves for the snapshot. They began to chat, and it turned out that she too was a stewardess, and insisted on another photo of the two of them, taken by her pilot boyfriend. They went off hoping they would meet again the next time their flights coincided in this way, and only when they were gone did Clemency realise that Lufthansa didn't fly to Beirut.

But CSA, the Czech airline, did.

She thought it over and left earlier than she'd planned, so she could arrive at the flat before the others. Denholm was surprised to see her, but when she told him about letting herself be photographed, perhaps by the Czech secret service, he laughed.

'That's a new one on me,' he said. 'I expect it's the brotherhood of the airlines that made you fall for it. Well, it's not so much of a surprise. If nothing else, it shows the opposition are interested in anyone on the Ahmar flight.'

'They're definitely involved, then?'

'Oh, I think so,' he said casually. 'I can't go into why, but we think there's a team of four in Jordan. A trade mission. Something to do with cotton. The Jordanians are being a bit cagey but I'm sure they have them taped.'

A team of four, supposedly there to promote trade. Just like in France. She could still see Petrov and his three colleagues at the reception desk in the hotel in Nice.

'We don't know who they are or what their intentions are, but we can be sure they aren't honourable,' Denholm said with his wry smile.

'There's one other thing,' she said. 'I don't want to mention this again in front of the others. But is there some way you could find out more about Mike Stannard?'

'I can ask London. He was checked out by Five, but there's no harm in digging a bit deeper. I take it something has made you suspicious?'

'Nothing new, but he's the only one who goes into the town in Ahmar. It's only to pick up his fruit, but if someone did want to make contact— '

'Fruit?'

'It's a silly thing he has of bringing some boxes of fruit back with each flight. It's to make some money on the side. It goes on to England on another airline. I think he and the other pilot split the profits.'

She tailed off. Denholm was staring at her in astonishment.

'This stuff goes onto the plane unchecked? Stannard just brings it on board and sticks it in the hold?'

'Oh, I see what you mean. I thought about that, but Stannard goes down to the *souk* himself and selects what he wants. I went with him one time. It's never the same things, so they couldn't know what he was going to buy and then slip a bomb into a watermelon. He even picks out the fruit he wants, and they go into open-sided crates or strong bags, so you couldn't add anything in without him noticing.'

'And the customs and so on, they don't do anything?'

'At Ahmar, it's leaving the country. At Beirut, it just transfers straight to another plane, so customs aren't involved.'

'But...'

Denholm ran his hand through his hair so that it stood up on end. It made him look even more shocked, and she had to stop herself from laughing.

'It would be very difficult to get anything out of the cargo hold in flight. You'd have to pull up the floor panels outside the cockpit and get to it that way. It wouldn't be possible to do it without the crew knowing.

'Why would he do that anyway?'

'Well, as the man at Farnborough said, the easiest way to hijack a plane is for one of the pilots to do it. Captain Macquarie would never do that. I just know. Stannard probably never would; but I don't know for sure. But anyway, if he wanted to bring a pistol on board, he could put it in his flight bag. No-one checks that. It's a big square kind of attaché case – at least as large as a doctor's bag – and they keep all their maps and flight plans in it. And their sandwiches and whisky if they feel like it.'

'You need to tell Farringdon about this. I'm sure you're right – God knows, you've got more of an interest in being right than any of us – but it's worth being sure. And you can't expect Farringdon to make the right decisions about the mission if they're not given all the facts.' He sighed. 'I can't understand why you haven't mentioned any of this during our meetings. That's what they're for.'

She hated being ticked off; particularly by someone whose good opinion she valued.

'No-one asked,' she said sullenly.

'Well, we can change that.'

Once the others had arrived, and they had reviewed progress and congratulated themselves on reaching the half-way point without incident, Denholm said that Clemency had obtained some fresh information to share – which was a kind way of putting it. She summed up what she'd told Denholm, and to her own ears it sounded rather good; using her initiative, keeping her eyes and ears open.

The four men each wore a different expression. Denholm was anxious, then relieved, as if watching a student give her first public recital. Farringdon was put out at the implicit criticism of the security arrangements in Ahmar, and that someone from Six should have pointed them out. But it was David's expression that was the surprise. She thought he'd be pleased that the people on the ground, the poor bloody infantry as he liked to call them, had come up with the goods. Instead, he looked like he wanted to murder her.

She didn't have long to find out why. As was now the habit, they went off for dinner after the meeting. She had wondered about ducking out, claiming a headache or an early start, but she knew that was pure cowardice. Instead, she found herself at a table in the Kit Kat Klub, while David was cold and resentful.

'I just can't understand why you didn't tell me. Why you had to come out with all of that in the meeting. Did you want me to look a complete fool?'

He emptied his glass; the waiter came over to refill it a second time.

'It wasn't like that,' she insisted. 'I was going— '

'You couldn't have just found out all of that. You didn't leave the plane today, so you can't have gone down to the *souk* with Stannard.'

'No, it was last week, but— '

'There you are! You could have told me last week, or any time today, but instead you saved it up for tonight, just to show them all how clever you are.'

'No, I— '

'I'm in charge of security on the plane. I should know about these things. Either you didn't give a moment's thought to where that leaves me, or how I would look; or you did, and you deliberately wanted to undermine me.'

'Of course I didn't. That's just ridiculous.'

'Is it? You're ambitious, aren't you? You've got your foot in the door with this Peter Aspinal business, and now you're worming your way in.'

'That's a horrible thing to say!'

'Is it? I wonder. Maybe you should take a good look at yourself in the mirror. You might not like what you see.'

'I've said I'm sorry. I didn't think any of it was important, but when I mentioned it to Denholm he insisted on bringing it up.'

'Did he,' David said, his voice flat with disbelief.

'If I'd known it mattered to you…'

'The thing that hurts the most is, I thought you cared. Because I don't think you realise how hard this job is. I'm on that plane, and I'm responsible for fifty lives. For four hours or more, any one of the passengers – or even the crew – could be on the point of trying to seize control, and I'd have a split second to decide what to do. If I get it wrong, all those people will die. All those hours, I can't do anything. I have to sit there and watch. It's like… Imagine you're in the trenches at the Somme, waiting for the whistle to go and you have to climb up out of the trenches and march forward to face the enemy fire. And imagine that whistle doesn't come, for hour after hour. What that does to the nerves. Then you have to do the whole bloody thing again, and again. D'you know what has kept me going? You. Watching you doing your job so calmly, smiling at the passengers and fetching them blankets and even taking that little runt Khalid up to the cockpit. About once every two minutes, for hour after hour, I think to myself that if Clemency can stand it, so can I. Because we're a team. Because we're on the same wavelength. Because maybe – just maybe – there's something else between us. And then this. I find you don't care. We're not a team. If you can make Clemency White look good, then David Fletcher can go screw himself.'

'That's simply not true,' she said, aghast to hear him pouring all this out.

'I tell you what. Let's just make it business, eh? Here.'

He plucked out some notes from his wallet.

'That should more than cover it. You enjoy your dinner. I'll see you at work tomorrow.'

With that, he stood and walked a little unsteadily out of the restaurant.

She sat, her face blazing with mortification, her eyes fixed on the bundle of notes he'd tossed so contemptuously onto the tablecloth. She couldn't look up. Every eye was on her; speculating, judging.

'Mam'zelle?' The waiter was standing over her. She had to look up; his expression had a hint of sympathy behind the formality. 'May I call you a taxi?'

It would allow her to escape with the illusion of dignity. All she wanted was to get home to the Rookery and cry. He must have planned the whole thing, from asking her to dinner to storming out and leaving her humiliated. The fact that he would want to do that to her hurt more than anything.

*

All along the sea front couples were walking hand in hand or chatting at tables, enjoying the evening breeze, the scent of the jacaranda trees, the glimpses of the sea and the setting moon beyond the seafront hotels.

She leant forward.

'Please could you stop at the next phone box.'

The taxi driver nodded, saying nothing. A moment later he had drawn to the side of the road and at once pulled out a folded newspaper and turned to the sports pages. She ran over to the phone box, taking some coins from her purse. The operator connected her to the airport switchboard, and she was soon speaking to the duty officer for CSA. She plunged into her explanation.

'I was supposed to meet one of your pilots tonight but I've stupidly forgotten the hotel where he's staying.'

'What is his name?'

'I'm not sure I should say…'

'It does not matter,' he replied, and Clemency could hear his smile down the telephone line. 'All the crew stay at the Intercontinental. I hope you have a most pleasant evening.'

With the taxi, she was there in five minutes. The hotel boutique was still open and she bought a headscarf and a pair of overlarge sunglasses, and a copy of *Vogue*, wondering if she'd even be able to claim back these expenses. Then she found a seat tucked out of sight in the lobby and sat down to wait. If the pilot and stewardess from CSA had been working for the enemy, she could turn the tables on them.

At first, she was troubled by how easy this might turn out to be. The GRU could have done the same, following her back to the Rookery and then on to the flat by the seafront to pick up the trail of Farringdon and the rest. Denholm had talked about hiding in plain sight, but surely they should be taking more precautions.

Time passed. People came and went, though none of them were pilots or cabin crew. She ordered a glass of wine and read about David Carradine and Barbara Harris, and how plaid was back for the winter. Then *Vogue* informed her that in the Fall of '65, *home was where the dream girls are, wearing what men adore – clothes that glow with the spirit of the evening – personal luxurious and highly decorative.* She turned to an interview with Bridget Riley, who hadn't followed the magazine's advice, but was photographed in clothes as severely monochrome as her paintings.

Then something made her look up. The lift doors opened as they had every few minutes for the last hour or more. The man who emerged glanced about him as he strode confidently across the lobby, taking in the couple at the check-in desk, the scattering of guests at the tables, even the boy at the piano, playing Cole Porter much too sweetly. Clemency felt his gaze pass over her, and she froze like a mouse under the shadow of a hawk. But he walked straight on.

There was nothing unusual about the man, nothing sinister or furtive. Just another Western businessman. The GRU had trained Petrov well.

# 18

Clemency hardly slept that night. Petrov was in Beirut. Farringdon was already planning his capture. If there were evidence of Petrov running an operation on Lebanese soil, the *Sûreté* could pick him up and hand him over to SIS. Within a few hours he could be RAF Akrotiri, on British soil. They would want time to debrief him, but the negotiations for his exchange with Peter would begin. He might be home by Christmas.

David was on the next day's flight to Ahmar as usual, but made a point of not speaking to her. It was frustrating because she wanted to know the latest about Petrov, but if sulking was his way of punishing her, then so be it. Maybe the five days that David was in Ahmar would help smooth things over.

She was under strict instructions not to contact Farringdon or even Denholm, but wait until the meeting the following week. She tried to distract herself with a couple of evenings out at one or other of the nightclubs with Felicity and some of the Pan Am crews. The dancing and throw-away conversation were exactly what she needed.

But as the week went on, the lack of news began to worry her. Farringdon may not have put himself out to keep her in the picture, but Denholm knew how much this mattered to her personally. Was he still away? What was Petrov up to? Had he slipped through their fingers? If he were still at large, then maybe they hadn't contacted her because it was safer for her that way. She'd been in Petrov's hands before, and though he'd thrown her back, he wouldn't make that mistake again. Worse, he now had a very personal grudge against her.

At last it was Tuesday and the flight to Ahmar. David seemed even more withdrawn as he boarded the plane. He didn't look at her, took his seat unsmiling, and there was alcohol on his breath. If he knew anything about Petrov, he wasn't going to share it with her. She'd have to wait for the briefing session that evening.

The flight was smooth, uneventful, except for her many various tasks and calls. Clemency was cleaning the toilet when the cockpit call chime went off. She washed and dried her hands and went to see what they wanted.

'What kept you?' Stannard snapped. 'Never mind. Ask your Mr Fletcher to come up here. There's an urgent message.'

She went to where David was sitting, gazing listlessly out of the window, chewing at his thumb. She touched his shoulder and he started. For a moment, she felt sudden sympathy for him. He wasn't well, and it wasn't just drinking too much. There was a red rash on the back of his hands, and traces of it at his throat too.

'Yes?'

There was such a look of hatred in his eyes that her anger returned.

'Captain Macquarie would like to speak to you in the cockpit,' she said coldly. 'Sir.'

Without another word, he stubbed out his cigarette and climbed out of his seat. No-one looked interested as they walked down the aisle together, though Clemency felt conspicuous. She showed him into the cockpit, and slipped in herself, hoping not to be noticed.

'Mr Fletcher? I'm Captain Macquarie. I've received a message for you. It makes it look like you're some kind of security man.'

'That's right.' David's voice was oddly flat, devoid of any emotion.

'Well, we're definitely in your hands, then. I'm advised that Bahrain ATC had a message phoned through that there's a bomb on board.'

He handed David a scrap of paper. He stared at it, unmoving, saying nothing.

In the end Macquarie coughed.

'Any advice, Mr Fletcher?'

'What? No. I…' He was chewing his thumb again. 'Where's the bomb?'

'We don't actually know,' Macquarie said patiently. 'It doesn't look as if the bomber was kind enough to tell us that.'

'Why tell us at all?' Clemency blurted out. When the three men turned to her, she had to plunge on.

'Why warn us? Maybe he wants a fuss. Have it in the newspapers. Maybe there's no bomb at all.'

'Can we risk it?'

'What would we do if we found it?' Stannard asked. 'Throw it out of the window?'

'We could disarm it,' Macquarie countered.

'We might end up setting it off.'

'Let's find it first. And while we argue the toss, let's get down to 10,000 feet. Then the bloody thing'll do a bit less damage. Oh, and where's the nearest field?'

'Ha'ir,' Stannard replied. 'About forty minutes.'

'We could divert. But as Caroline says, that might be what they want.'

'Does it matter?' Stannard said. 'At least we'd be on the ground.'

Clemency expected David to say something; anything. Instead he kept looking at the floor, scratching the back of his hand.

'Mr Fletcher?'

'Another message,' Stannard said, holding his hand up for quiet as he jotted it down. 'It says the bomb's in the luggage of the passenger in seat 11C.'

'11C?' David said. 'Really? 11C?'

David began to chuckle to himself, his eyes fixed on the floor, a strange, secret smile on his face. The two pilots stared at him in consternation. Then it became much worse, the laughter becoming hysterical, peal upon peal, his head thrown back, tears coming to his eyes.

She touched David's arm and he stopped, then stared at her as if he had never seen her before. Then he pushed her aside and stumbled out of the cockpit. They heard the door of the toilet shut with a slam.

Macquarie was the first to break the silence.

'Well, he's no bloody James Bond, is he? Looks like it's for us to sort out. Who's in 11C? Caroline, can you fetch the passenger list?'

But there was no need. 11C was David's seat.

*

They had the access hatch up and Clemency was ready to climb down into the baggage hold. As she had said, they had to try and find it. It might explode any minute, or might even have a reversed barometric switch, so it would detonate as the plane came into land. Macquarie hadn't disagreed, though he gave her an odd look as she reeled off this knowledge of the ways of saboteurs. They'd had a gallant exchange about who should descend into the hold and find David's bag, but Clemency had insisted. Not only were the two men both at least six feet tall; if the bomb did explode, it might still be possible to save the plane. But for that, they would need the skill of both pilots.

She dropped the few feet to the floor of the plane, her feet resting on its skin. The noise was much louder, and it was cold too, and she crawled between boxes of machinery and bundles of wires to reach the baggage compartment. It was full almost to the ceiling and she had to worm her way in, and then began to check the nearest cases. The names were hand-written, and in the dark, lit only by a torch, the pressure of time tore at her nerves. There would be at least forty suitcases to check. Unless she were lucky, she'd be there when they landed.

Or when it went off.

The passengers above might survive, might have an extra few minutes of life before the stricken plane hit the ground. She would be dead, what was left of her spilled from the shattered plane, along with the rest of the luggage. They might never find her. Or maybe, in fifty years, someone would pass by and see the remains, the bones and scraps of cloth.

All the time she kept searching, methodically piling the checked cases to one side, until there was a patch of turbulence and the whole lot came down on top of her.

She struggled to lift them off, on the edge of panic as their weight made it hard to breathe. Of all the ways to die…

She broke through to the surface and began to check again. And as if it were time for her luck to change, the very next bag was the one.

Locked.

She squirmed back to the door and called up.

'I've found it. I need some pliers.'

'Are you sure?' Stannard's voice was worried.

'It's for the lock.'

After a moment, his hand appeared and she grabbed the tool. With that, it only took a moment to cut through the lock and open up the case. She pulled out David's shirts, suits, pants, the washbag, shoes and ties, until the case was empty. She even turned it upside down, weighed it. Nothing. No bomb.

The only thing that looked suspicious was a handsomely wrapped parcel about half the size of a shoe box. She sniffed it, and it smelt of perfume. It was far too light to be a bomb. Tugging away at the paper, she saw it was a cardboard box, and pulling that apart, she drew out a pair of black silk pyjamas and a card. On the card a single word in capitals: BOOM!

She turned over and stared up at the metal of the ceiling, a few inches above her nose. This was the only place to be alone on the plane. She could think it through here better than anywhere.

Someone knew about David. They wanted him warned off – though they couldn't have predicted just how effective that would turn out to be.

But why? If he'd been spotted, why not leave him in place? Why risk them bringing in a replacement they wouldn't know?

And why had he lost his mind like that?

She began to work her way back to the hatch. There was nothing for them to do until they were on the ground. But then, she'd need to talk to Vaughn. The operation was blown. The security around the Emir was compromised. The bomb could have been real, and everyone on board the flight would have died. Yet for some reason, the whole thing had been a hoax.

None of it made sense; and that was the most frightening thing of all.

# 19

Macquarie had called ahead on the Red Air company frequency to arrange for a doctor to meet the plane and for the British Embassy to be informed. The latter was at Clemency's suggestion, and she stood uneasily under their speculative gaze. Stannard's was suspicious, Macquarie's something else entirely, a mix of anger and anxiety and perhaps a hint of betrayal for not squaring with him and so putting the passengers in danger.

An hour later, they were on the ground, the plane parked at the arrivals gate, and the engines winding down. Felicity accompanied the passengers to immigration. Only then had they used a screwdriver to open the door to the washroom, where David sat crouched over on the floor, his back to the bulkhead.

They'd tried coaxing him out, to no effect; and then the doctor arrived and produced a syringe, and she'd heard David's screeches and glimpsed his staring eyes and bared teeth over the shoulders of the men, and it had taken Stannard's weight and the doctor's experience to sedate him.

In the end an ambulance drove out to the plane and they loaded him onto it in a stretcher. The two orderlies had a strange calmness to them and were strongly built beneath their white clothes. She had an image of a vast and souless asylum, of long bleak corridors echoing to meaningless screams.

Long after the ambulance had left the field, Clemency walked over to the terminal and sat for a while in the crew room, trying to contain her distress. Then Farzana arrived from her flight from Teheran. After one look at Clemency, she asked if she'd be all right to fly the next day, or if they should try and find a replacement.

'I'll be fine,' Clemency insisted. 'It was just such a shock.'

'Felicity told me all about it. A horrible practical joke.'

'That's right.' As an explanation, it had the advantage of being fairly close to the truth.

'And it was the passenger who asked you out?'

It was unusual for Farzana to be insensitive, and Clemency wished she'd leave her alone. But then again, she hadn't been there, and couldn't imagine how awful it had been.

'Did he tell you he was scared of flying?

'No, we talked about other things. He was a bit dull, really. I never expected anything like this.'

'Had he been drinking?'

'He just went to pieces. After that, we were too busy to do anything with him. We left him in the lavatory.'

It was a relief when it was Clemency's turn to give a statement to the Lebanese Civil Aviation Authority, and she could bring Farzana's interrogaton to an end. She went through the whole story again, while the two officials wrote it down, giving nothing away. She was the last of the crew to be interviewed, and as they left they told her to wait for an official of the *Sûreté*. It was more than an hour before a Captain Auer arrived, powerfully-built and impatient, not someone to cross. He asked her to repeat her story, then questioned her about David, and her replies didn't convince him.

'But how did you know he was a security man? Did he talk of this to you?'

'No, but I thought he must be. He was carrying a gun, for one thing. A lawyer with the Foreign Office wouldn't do that.'

'Why did you not tell your captain that there was a man with a gun on board? He tells me he had no idea.'

'I thought it would cause trouble.'

Auer was dissatisfied and kept covering the same ground. Might he lose patience and take her to the police station for more interrogation? And if he did, who would come to her aid? Denholm? Farringdon? Or would they think that she was an embarrassment and leave her to look after herself? It had happened before.

In the end, another officer brought a message and he left. Time passed. Clemency realised that she was tired and hungry and thirsty. She hadn't been told she had to stay, and there was no guard on the door; but she had only begun to wonder what would happen if she did leave the room when Auer returned.

'Good. You are free to go.' His stern gaze now held a hint of amusement. 'And thank you for being so... professional in our discussion.' He saluted her with a trace of irony and left.

Someone, presumably Denholm, had explained who she was. She waited for a few minutes, readying herself to return to the crew room. Reliving the experience had been so horrible: she couldn't help thinking of David crouched in the washroom, sweating, unable to look anyone in the eye, not recognising her. In those moments, David had been something less than human.

She thought too of the way the ambulance doors

had closed on him; and how she would probably never see him again. A casualty of the mission, just as surely as if he had been gunned down on the street.

The others were in the crew room, waiting for her to finish, but she couldn't face a drink in the airport bar with any of them, even Macquarie. She walked through the departures hall – quiet at this time of the evening – to the main entrance. At once a Peugeot taxi sped up beside her, its window down.

'M'selle Green?' The driver was young, with carefully styled hair. The radio in the car was playing *Good Vibrations* and he was tapping the side of the car in time, very pleased with life.

She got into the back and the car roared away, pressing her into her seat. The run into the city might be even more nerve-racking than usual, but at least it would be quicker than the bus.

Then they turned off the main road into one of the southern suburbs. Perhaps it was a short cut. Or perhaps…

She sat up. How could she have simply stepped into the taxi like that? She hadn't checked the message, or the driver's credentials. She'd assumed that someone – perhaps Rossiter – had been thoughtful about how exhausted she'd be after the questioning and had arranged the car for her. But of course, that was entirely out of character.

They were speeding through narrow streets, blank-faced houses to each side.

'Where are we going?' she asked. The man shrugged, then rattled off some words, none of which meant much, but which could have been the name of their destination or of whoever was waiting there.

She sat back, trying to think what to do. Open the

door and jump out? They were going far too fast, and he'd simply slam on the brakes and then come and look for her. Already they were in the hills above the city. She was surprised by just how empty it felt, dark, no other traffic, with Beirut only fifteen minutes away, its lights still visible beyond the edge of the road.

She tried again, and again he talked back at her in Arabic, saying something that sounded like Bay Marie, repeated several times, all with a reassuring smile. And then her mind cleared and she realised he was speaking in heavily-accented French. Soon she had established that the car was to take her to see *Monsieur Denom*. Denholm must have thought of the risk that the entire mission was blown, and arranged a safer place to meet than the seafront flat.

The villa was down a long track that passed between high stone walls, so that it might have led to a farm in Cornwall, save for the outline of olive trees to each side, and the faint clank of bells from a herd of sheep or perhaps goats that floated down from the hills when she stepped from the car. She turned to the driver, but he waved to show it was already paid for.

The youth who answered the door welcomed her in Arabic and gestured for her to follow. It was pleasantly cool in the tiled hall. Denholm appeared and led her into a room with plain white walls, rich rugs on a wooden floor and sofas arranged round an open fire. She loved it at once, and realised it was the first proper Lebanese house she had entered. But any chance to explore would have to wait.

Farringdon, Denholm; it made David's absence all the more obvious.

'You drink red wine, don't you, Clemency?' he said, as if trying to make it all less intimidating; but this would be a kind of interrogation; and as soon as she was settled, Farringdon asked her to go through the whole story, in as much detail as she could. But though she tried to make her account clear and succinct, and as factual as she could, he was still dissatisfied.

She'd finished by explaining that she'd asked Macquarie to radio ahead so that there would be someone to meet them and spirit David away, rather than hand him over to the airport doctors. Now she wondered if this was some kind of breach of security.

In the end, Farringdon broke the silence.

'When you went to tell him there was a message for him, what was he doing?'

'Looking out of the window.'

'Did he see you approach him?'

'Yes, but he didn't respond or say anything until I stopped by him.'

'How did he seem?'

She hesitated. 'Just the same as always. Maybe a bit on edge.'

'Had he been drinking?'

'Oh, no.'

Why had she said that? Some stupid idea of loyalty to David?

'What about his skin? Was he sweating? Or off colour?'

'No.'

'Or his eyes? Did his pupils look dilated?'

'I don't think so. I mean, I think I would have noticed, and I didn't.'

She told herself not to get flustered; but it was hard not to feel that in some way she was to blame.

'When he followed you, did he walk all right?'

'He was fine. And I followed him.'

'Did anyone touch him when he walked down the aisle? Or did he stop for any reason?'

'No.'

'You're sure.'

'Yes.'

She realised now how his thinking was going; that David had been got at in some way; poison or drugs. But though Farringdon took her through every detail of the next two or three minutes, she could only say that David had looked in control until the first mention of the bomb; and after hearing it was in his bag, he had gone to pieces.

'How did the two pilots take the news about the bomb?' Vaughn asked.

'They were worried, of course.'

'And you? How did you feel?'

'I was scared.'

'But all three of you could carry on. They could fly the plane. You, of course, climbed into the baggage hold and established that the bomb threat was a hoax. I'm just wondering if you have any explanation for why Mr Fletcher took the news so differently.'

'His nerve broke. I'm sorry to have to say it, but that's what happened.'

They digested this silently.

'How did the Soviets know about David?' she asked. 'They must have agents in Ahmar. I mean, how would they get it into his luggage otherwise?'

'Surely that shows the conspiracy is home-grown in Ahmar,' Farringdon replied. 'We know the Soviets have no presence there.'

'But what about Petrov and his team?'

'The *Sûreté* made enquiries at the hotel,' Vaughn said. 'There was no-one answering to your description of this man Petrov staying there. Of course, a lot of business people come and go, and I'm not saying you made a mistake, but there is certainly no GRU unit operating in Beirut at the moment.'

'But I saw him,' she protested.

Farringdon and Vaughn exchanged a glance. They didn't need to say anything. *The girl's overwrought. Seeing what she wants to see. Obsessed with Petrov because of Peter Aspinal. We'll just have to humour her.*

She looked at Denholm, but however sympathetic he might be – and he had his pained expression on, as if sharing her frustration – he showed no sign of coming to her aid.

'So,' Farringdon said. 'My own view is that Mohammad doesn't want to blow up the plane – otherwise he'd have put a real bomb on board, not a fake. But he wanted David removed from the plane, and the obvious reason for that is that it would make a hijacking easier. Our hand is weakened, because we don't have David on board. But it's also strengthened, because we have a better idea of what we're dealing with. The Emir's treatment is to finish in just over a a week's time. So we have the return flight to Ahmar on Thursday, then one more round trip. Can we keep things going that long.

'Do you have someone to take David's place?' Denholm asked.

'We don't. We've a couple of bodyguard types we could use, but I'm not sure that's what the operation needs. And they'd be a bit obvious. How about you?'

'Not for something like this. But doesn't the continuation of the operation rather depend on Miss White?'

'That's a good point.' Farringdon turned almost formally to Clemency. 'Whoever the opposition is, they spotted Mr Fletcher and used this hoax to send him a warning. I'm sure they had no idea it would work so spectacularly, but there we are. It still shows that they are aware of our efforts to protect the Emir. That increases the hazards of your own role.'

'What will you do if I drop out? I mean, will the Emir keep flying?'

'Yes, there's no doubt about that.'

She didn't look at Denholm. He'd want her to stop. But she had a new loyalty: to Macquarie, Felicity, Farzana, and even Stannard. She couldn't walk away and leave them in danger. That mattered more than the Emir, or his family, or even the other passengers who would be killed along with them.

'Then I'll carry on.'

# 20

The flight to Ahmar passed in a daze for Clemency. She could carry out her duties, but felt dissociated from herself, from the others, from the passengers. Everything from the galley ovens to the cabin door levers looked insubstantial, as if they might break off in her hand or crumble into dust. All that seemed real was David's face, raging and fearful like an animal in a trap, as they'd led him away.

She had cleared the meals and served the coffee and liqueurs and it was the one time on the flight where she could think to rest for a few moments. She poured herself a cup of coffee and sat in the jump seat, closing her eyes and letting the noise of the engines become a lullaby and the vibration and gentle massage rising through the soles of her feet and running through the tired muscles of her back.

But there was someone standing over her: the Emir's daughter, Fatima.

'I'm so sorry to disturb you,' she said. 'I have become used to coming here and talking to your colleague Farzana.'

'That's all right, Your Highness. Would you like some coffee?'

'Tea, please. It may seem rude of me to say, when we are looked after so well on these flights, but this is not coffee. It is like water.'

Clemency smiled ruefully.

'I don't know how we'd make Arabic coffee properly in the galley. You have to boil it over a stove, don't you?'

'You have to roast the beans over a fire first. I do not think the captain would approve.'

As Clemency prepared the tea, she asked after Khalid.

'I hope he's having a good holiday. He was so looking forward to it.'

'Last week he shot a gazelle,' Fatima replied with a touch of pride. 'It took him many hours, and then he did...' she lacked the words in English. 'All the preparation...' She laughed. 'I want to say surgery.... all that was necessary to bring it back.'

'I have cousins in Scotland who hunt deer,' Clemency said. 'I think the word is gralloching.'

'Is it? Anyway, to go to England and learn Latin is good, but it matters very much to our people that he should prove himself in this way.'

'It's a shame it's so far away. You must miss him.'

'There is nowhere else he can learn. If you wish to know the gazelle, you go to the desert and you follow its tracks, you see how it moves. If you wish to know the English, you must go to England and you must watch them closely.'

It was Clemency's turn to smile, but Fatima was quite serious.

'When the English first came, they did not bring much and they did not demand much from us. But that has changed. The oil has changed it. Look at Kuwait. Iraq decides it will invade, and only the British made them stop. Kuwait is right to be grateful to your people. But they are paying for that, are they not? British Petroleum has the contracts it wants to extract the oil.'

'That's what someone told me on the first day I arrived. Everything comes back to oil.'

'Perhaps,' Fatima said. 'Oil and pride. We do not have anything else.'

*

After the return flight to Beirut, the same taxi driver was waiting to take her to what she now guessed was Denholm's own house. In daylight, she could take in the wonderful location and the sense of peace it brought, to be so close to the city, yet so high above it.

Farringdon and Denholm had been there for hours, judging by the state of the ash trays. There were empty coffee cups, and the scent of whisky. They had been joined by Major Hereward from the Residency in Ahmar, in a civilian suit but still straight-backed and military.

Denholm poured drinks without being asked. Clemency took a sip and at once felt hungry and realised she hadn't eaten since breakfast.

'Shall we bring Miss White up to speed?' Denholm began.

'We've got a bit more gen on this business,' Hereward replied. Out of uniform, he looked ill at ease; or perhaps it was what he had to say.

'The message was telephoned to the control tower about an hour after the plane took off. There was a bit of shilly-shallying about whether they had the authorisation to pass it on, which is why it was almost another hour until you got it. The controller says it was an Arabic voice, but not an Ahmari.'

He took a sip of his drink.

'We've traced the package. It seems Mr Fletcher had been, er, making use of the services of a brothel in Ahmar. Going at least two or three times a week over the last month.'

Clemency felt the blood draining from her face.

'He always saw the same girl. She was the one who gave him the pyjamas as a gift. She, er, told him that she missed him when he was in Beirut each week, and wanted him to have something to remember her by. When we questioned her, she said it was another client who put it up to her. He told her he wanted a favour from Fletcher and he thought this would help. He bought the pyjamas and showed them to her before he wrapped them up. And he made a point of telling her to insist that Fletcher didn't open it until he reached his hotel room in Beirut.'

'So she knew it was harmless,' Vaughn confirmed.

'Oh yes, otherwise she would surely have wondered what was going on. It could have been smuggling, for example. She's not a stupid girl by any means.'

'What about this man?'

'An Iraqi engineer, working on one of the surveys. Coincidentally he flew out of Ahmar on Tuesday, on the Gulf Air flight to Karachi.'

'And from thence to Mother Russia?' Vaughn asked rhetorically. 'Maybe via Kabul? It's tempting to think so. But maybe a little obvious?'

'Inconclusive, I'd say,' Denholm offered. 'If you wanted to throw suspicion on the Soviets, that's what you'd do, isn't it?'

'I think we can exclude Soviet activity in Ahmar itself,' Hereward said defensively.

'If it wasn't them, then what was it all about?'

'It was a warning,' Hereward said decisively.

'They realised our security was too good, so they wanted to scare us – scare the Emir – into changing his arrangements.'

Farringdon nodded judiciously, though it wasn't clear if he accepted Hereward's logic, or was admiring his skill in turning this fiasco to his advantage.

'What I can't understand,' Hereward went on, 'is why Fletcher went to pieces. That can't have been any part of the plan. Miss White, you saw him that day. Was he worried? On edge?'

'He didn't say much when he got on board. He certainly looked preoccupied. Tired, as well.'

He would, she thought bitterly, if he spent his nights with this other girl.

'But you weren't worried about him?'

'No.'

Yet that wasn't true. Ever since the night in Ahmar, on the battlements, his moods had been hard to read; friendly one day, distant the next, but all the time more and more withdrawn into himself, no longer seeing the mission as a challenge, but something to be endured. Perhaps if she'd shown him a little more sympathy…

'What will happen to him now?' she asked.

'He's in a sanitorium in the north, just outside Baalbek. Very good place. We'll give him a couple of weeks there and then he'll go home. By ship, of course.'

'Would it help if I went to see him?'

For a moment, Farringdon hesitated. Then he said he thought it wasn't a good idea, and she was ashamed to feel such relief.

That seemed to be the cue for Clemency to go; no doubt the men would continue discussing it all into the night. Denholm came with her to the door and waited while the driver was summoned. It was a beautiful evening, cool, the stars clear beyond the line of the palms and, far off, Beirut was reduced to a spray of twinkling lights.

'So what did happen to David? Only you looked like you could have said a lot more.'

She sighed. Peter had once said that everyone only had a limited amount of courage, and that if you used it up too freely, it could become exhausted and let you down. Maybe that was what had happened to David. She doubted she would ever find out for sure. But whatever the truth, she couldn't help him now.

'What would it matter what I said? They know. "Lack of Moral Fibre." That's what will go on his report, won't it?'

He didn't reply.

'Who do you think is behind the plot?' she asked abruptly. 'Only we're seven weeks in and they still don't know. Or won't tell me.'

'What I think hardly matters. I've never even been to Ahmar.'

'But what do you think?'

'Me?' he replied with his sad, lopsided smile. 'I think we should forget the politics. They're children. The Emir is their father. That's where the answer lies.'

'Really?' She wasn't convinced. 'How does that help? Who do you think it is?'

'Suleiman.' He said it reluctantly, and yet as if it were obvious. 'He's the youngest, the child who must have everyone's attention. If he were a Teddy Boy, wielding a flick-knife on Brighton beach, he'd be a juvenile delinquent. But it's the same human nature. He reacts against his father, his family, by going to an extreme. With him, it isn't rockers and mopeds, it's seizing on religion and taking it to the most fundamentalist form.

That has a logic or a momentum to it that might lead him into plotting against his own father.'

'Would he go through with it?'

'Would any of them? Maybe having Khalid as a nephew doesn't help. Suleiman's no longer even the favoured youngest son.'

'But surely the Soviets are behind this. They wouldn't be involved with Suleiman.' It scared her that even Denholm wasn't taking Petrov seriously.

The car pulled up beside her.

'I'm sorry, Clemency.'

He helped her into the car and watched as she drove off. Only then did she wonder why he had apologised to her.

*

It was still early when she was dropped off at the Rookery. She went up to her room, not looking forward to an evening on her own, thinking too much. When Felicity came in, insisting that she should join her for a night out, it was hard to resist.

'Gemal said I had to make you come along. He has a friend who wants to meet you.'

A friend. Clemency still had her suspicions about what else the friend would want. But if there was a chance of finding out more, however slim, she had to take it.

They met Gemal at the Kit Kat. The man he was drinking with – a bottle of Johnny Walker Black Label very prominent on their table – turned out not to be the mystery friend, but another business associate; and this was a relief. He had looked greedily at the two women as they approached; and he was at least fifty and heavily paunched. They chatted for a little, had a drink, and then Clemency and Felicity went to dance. The music was a bit dated, with Chubby Checker still twisting and Little Eva still locomoting, and not nearly loud enough, but at least it was familiar.

She was becoming used to the way that, in the Beirut clubs, the men ranged around the room liked to watch the women dance, and it wasn't hard to imagine what they were thinking; but she could ignore that and enjoy herself. It was better than the alternative, those cabarets that she'd been to a few times, once with David and once with another friend of Felicity's, where she would sit at a little table while the man she was with watched the professional dancers go through their routines, and she had to pretend not to know what they were dreaming about.

Hot and breathless, they made their way back to their table to find Gemal's business contact had gone, and in his seat a much younger man, with a neat moustache and an uneasy look in his eyes. This was Michel, the one who was supposed to know something secret about Red Air. They chatted about nothing much for a while, and there was more dancing, but Clemency couldn't find a way to draw Michel out. In fact, he didn't seem particularly interested in her, despite Felicity's insistence that the four of them should meet up.

Soon she found herself on the dance floor with Gemal, which wasn't at all the idea; though she found she was coming to like him. He danced very well, and though he played up to the image of the international playboy, he had a sense of humour. Michel, in contrast, must have had a fair amount to drink before arriving, and kept on working his way through the bottle of whisky. Gemal and Felicity went off to dance, but he declined her suggestion they do the same.

'So you fly for Red Air? Like the other girl?'

'I do. Are you one of our regulars?'

'I would not fly with anyone else.'

'You must know a lot about the airline. Probably more than I do.'

'I do.' His smile was unsettling.

'We often have passengers who think they know all the tricks. The best seats and so on.'

He rose to her bait.

'Oh no, I know more than that. I am in the Club.'

She took refuge in her drink, puzzling what he might mean. The way he had said it, the Club would have been something she ought to know about.

'How long for?' she ventured.

'Since it began. But I had already met Monsieur Rossiter in Cyprus.'

Perhaps Michel was one of his early investors.

'Do you go to the Club often?'

'Enough.' So at least it was a place. 'I have never seen you there, though. A pity.'

'They work me too hard.'

This had some inner meaning for Michel. His eyes took on more interest, as if she were flirting with him.

'You must come one day when I am there. We will have some proper fun then.'

'I'd like that,' she said, wondering what she was committing herself to. But she was saved from more of this double-speak by the others returning. Felicity signalled for her to come to the bathroom. At least one of them was enjoying herself.

'He likes you,' she insisted. 'I can tell.'

'Felicity, he can't even remember which of us is which.'

'Well, maybe...'

There was more dancing, then more drinks, and all on an empty stomach. She found it hard not to yawn, and she promised herself one more go at getting Michel to open up and then she would slip away.

'What is the favourite place you fly to with us?'

'I have many business interests, you know, in Istanbul and Cairo and Teheran.'

'I mainly fly on the route down to Ahmar. Do you ever go there?'

'Never. I know Prince Mohammed. A very good friend. Very good. If I wanted to do business in Ahmar, I would call on him, no problem. But there is nothing there. No business.'

'Won't the oil change that?'

'Maybe. But for me, I go where the money is now, not five years. The whole Gulf, it is nothing. Except Kuwait, perhaps.'

'What's Cairo like?' It was the only place he'd mentioned with a Communist link.

'Good for business. Since they nationalised the oil, there is more money about. Less is going to London and New York. Times are good there.'

Still she was making no progress. She went back to asking about this club, but he was more interested in the cigarette girl making her way around the tables. He waved her over and bought a packet of Camels, then watched her appraisingly, head a little on one side, as she walked away. Clemency decided to do the same. She found Felicity, wished her well for the evening, and went to find a cab.

# 21

It was still dark when Clemency was shaken awake. She sat up, confused. It took her a moment to realise it was Farzana, outlined against the faint light from the street lamps outside.

'What is it?'

'The police. Downstairs. They are asking for you.'

She wrapped herself in a dressing gown and followed Farzana down to the hall where two uniformed police officers were waiting.

'Miss Green? You are to come with us, please.'

'What is it? What's happened?'

'Everything will be explained.'

They spoke in French and were perfectly civil; but the air was thick with their power, just as if they had kicked down the door. Behind her, on the stairs, Clemency could sense the others watching her, speculating on what she had done.

'May I see your identity papers?' Farzana asked them. They were surprised, on the edge of turning to anger, but after exchanging a glance they shrugged and took out their warrants; a card and a badge in a small leather wallet. Clemency peered at them over Farzana's shoulder. She'd never seen one before, of course, but it looked like the real thing.

They allowed her a few minutes to dress. By then, the other residents of the Rookery had gone back to bed, except for Farzana.

'Would you like me to come with you?'

'No, I'm fine. But could you call my godfather? He'd want to know. His name is Charles Denholm. He's in the phone book.'

They had the door open to hurry her along, and in a few moments she was in the back of a car and speeding through the empty streets. Her thoughts were jumbled together. Had the Lebanese authorities realised she was there under a false identity? How smart of Farzana to check their papers – something she should have thought of herself. Was she right to involve Denholm? Had the Soviets tipped the Lebanese off to remove her from the mission?

She had some idea they were heading into the southern suburbs, just off the main road to the airport. Then they drew up at the side of the road, where there was a cluster of police cars by a half-built villa in a patch of waste ground, steel supporting rods sprouting from the raw concrete of the frame. Someone had set up floodlights, so that it looked a little like a film set; everyone gathered around something she couldn't make out.

The two policemen led her from the car down a rough track, towards the lights. Now it felt like they'd arrived late for a party, with people heading for the cars and preparing to leave. An ambulance inched its way past. A shortish man in uniform waved her over.

There were introductions that she didn't quite take in, because she was still sleepy.

'You are from Red Air?'

'Yes.'

'You were out last night?'

Only then did the pieces begin to fall into place. This was a crime scene. The ambulance. A face missing from the crowd in the Rookery.

'Is it Felicity? Has something happened to her?'

He nodded.

'But I saw her a few hours ago,' she protested. 'She was fine.'

'I am sorry. Your friend is dead.'

*

The mortuary was in the pathology building of the American Hospital. The smell of wood polish and formaldehyde took her back to her childhood, when she had gone into the hospital from time to time with her father. The building had the same high windows to give the maximum light; the same dark wooden cases along the walls to hold specimens, equipment, textbooks behind tall glass doors. The students, too, were strolling around, proud of their white coats, just as they had been in the Dorchester Hospital. They glanced at her, first appraising her, perhaps wondering if she were the daughter of one of the lecturers – and then realising the reason for her visit, and that chatting her up was unlikely to get very far.

What made it obvious was the man at his side; Captain Auer, who had taken down her statement about the events of the night before.

They paused at the door of the mortuary.

'Have you seen a dead body before, Miss Green?'

'Yes, I have. I'll be fine.'

But she wasn't. Felicity had been so very alive; and now she was dead. There was no trace of fear or pain or suffering on her features. There was nothing there at all. She was gone, and all that was left had the cold dead look of raw clay.

*

Once they were finished with her, and her statement was typed and checked and signed, she went to meet Denholm at the flat. She'd kept her composure, but once she saw his anxious face, she began to sob, and she buried her face into the shoulder of his linen suit, and he patted her back diffidently and tried to soothe her. Eventually he had sat her down and pushed a glass of whisky into her hand. The spirit was harsh on her empty stomach, and made her feel light-headed, which was exactly what she wanted.

'I hate this city,' she said between gulps. 'How could they do that. They killed her, you know.'

'Who?'

'Those horrible men. All the time, watching us, and playing with us, and thinking we'd do whatever they pleased. Unless it was all planned. Unless they wanted to kill her.'

'Why would they do that?'

'That's what they're like. They're... evil. Sick. They see a European girl and all they can think of is...'

She dissolved into tears, vaguely conscious of Denholm standing over her.

'Is that what you told the police?'

She nodded.

'They say Gemal and Michel have alibis,' she said. 'They left her waiting for a taxi and went back into the club. But that's not true. They must have taken her somehow and—'

'Clemency, listen to me. You're upset, and you're not thinking clearly. It wasn't them. It was the opposition.'

'But why would they…?'

'Why would Gemal? This idea that every man in Beirut wants to rape a Western girl – it's just nonsense. Say he'd made a pass at her, and she'd turned him down. He'd be angry, he'd be disappointed. Just like a Westerner. Why would he kill her? Or if she threatened to tell someone, why would he care? He's not married. She can't blackmail him, so she's not in any danger from that. So you might say, then he's a psychopath. What are the chances of that?'

'But she's dead.'

'Yes. And I'm saying, look beyond what we're being asked to believe. It's too simple. Look, I've asked around. No-one thinks Gemal is the kind of man to do this. They might all be wrong, but he's thirty and if this was what he was like, surely it would have come out by now.'

'He's being protected.'

'Yes, but when you protect someone in this society, you are using up a lot of favours. Even if you never stand trial, it's not cost-free. If he's thirty, and he's a sex maniac, then this won't be the first time. He'd have a reputation. Probably the family would have found some way to keep him out of harm's way.'

'What are you saying?'

'They didn't want her, they wanted you. Either to interrogate or to kill.'

'Petrov?'

'Maybe. It might be the Ahmaris, but this wouldn't be easy for them to set up. Your friend Gemal was being used to get you to be somewhere at a fixed time and place, with not too many witnesses around and a ready-made explanation for your disappearance.'

As soon as he said it, the pieces fell into place.

Gemal had pressed Felicity to bring her English friend along. Gemal had probably been asked to do this by Michel, who was probably paying off a debt to someone else, a chain of favours leading back to whoever had arranged the killing. When they came out of the nightclub with Felicity, the watchers picked her up instead of Clemency.

'When did they find out they'd got the wrong one?' she asked.

'I don't know. Maybe they tried to get her to talk. They would have known soon enough. Or maybe it was all about killing you, and they didn't realise until the next day.'

Clemency put her hands over her mouth. She couldn't stop thinking of what Felicity's last moments must have been like.

'I'm sorry...'

Tears wouldn't help bring her back; but they were still running down her cheeks. She shook her head in frustration.

'Come on, old thing,' Denholm said, embarrassed by her show of emotion. 'We need to talk to Vaughn. I'm going to ask him to fly you home.'

'Why?'

'This whole operation is a fiasco. First the hoax bomb and now this. The other side have spotted both of you and taken you out of the game. I think you're right. It must be the Soviets. It's too... too effective for some amateur mob of conspirators. The business with the photo at the Club. They were Czech, weren't they? That must have been how they identified you. Or maybe they saw you with Vaughn. Or with me. Maybe it doesn't matter now. The damage is done.'

'I'm not going back.'

'You're marked, Clemency. If Moscow have agreed you can be eliminated, they will try again, you can be sure of that.'

'There's only another week. I can stay somewhere else. You can have me driven to the airport in a tank, if you like. But I'm not letting them beat us.'

'Because it's Petrov?'

'If you like.'

Denholm sighed in frustration.

'We'll tell Vaughn. Let him make the final decision.'

'No. There's no reason to tell him anything. All we have is suspicion. No facts.'

'That's going too far.'

There was an unfamiliar edge to Denholm's voice. In the end, Clemency nodded her agreement.

'Look,' he said, sympathetic again. 'How about this?'

He grabbed a pad and began to write.

> FELICITY LANE BRITISH CITIZEN REDAIR STEWARDESS AHMAR FLIGHTS MURDERED LAST NIGHT BEIRUT. POSSIBLE MISTAKEN IDENTITY. WHITE PREPARED CONTINUE ASSIGNMENT TO COMPLETION. ADVISE. DENHOLM.

'How is that?'

'That's fair.' She stared at the words for a long time. 'Thank you.'

'Please don't thank me, Clemency. I could be signing your death warrant.'

*

She lay on the bed, with the light off, looking out over

the jumble of roofs to the moonlit sky and the deep mass of the mountains. She couldn't get the image of Felicity out of her mind; or rather, the Felicity who had almost dragged her to the club, who just wanted to go out and dance and have a drink and maybe a chaste kiss with Gemal, if she had felt like it; and instead had been snatched from the street, and been frightened, and then hurt, and then killed.

It was Petrov. It had to be.

It was ridiculous to think of individuals, of a rivalry between herself and Petrov, with the thousands of tanks and planes and millions of soldiers lined up on each side of the Iron Curtain, the state bureaucracies, the political blocs, and the rest of it. Yet this was personal. Felicity was just a bystander, killed because Petrov couldn't take the time to come up with a plan that worked. To kill when there was no alternative was one thing. To kill to cover up your incompetence was unforgivable.

There had been a time when Petrov was at her mercy. She could have finished him and walked away and no-one would have known. She had chosen to spare him.

Now, Felicity was dead. She would not make the same mistake again.

# 22

In the grey light of dawn, the four of them assembled by the plane: Macquarie and Stannard in their black and white uniforms, Clemency and Farzana in red. Macquarie looked old and sick, Stannard even more withdrawn than usual, and Farzana was furious, as if she had been insulted. Clemency wondered how she looked to them; guilty, perhaps, for leaving Felicity alone at the bar.

'I suppose I should say something,' Macquarie said slowly. 'God knows what, though.'

'Do they know anything more?' Stannard asked. 'Any leads?'

They all looked at Clemency.

'I don't know,' she said, on the edge of desperation. Maybe she wouldn't be able to manage the flight after all.

'I won't say anything stupid like how it's what she'd want us to do,' Macquarie said heavily. 'But we've got a flight to make and we've got to keep our minds on the job. If any of us can't do that, we should stand down. There's no shame attached. Rossiter will understand.'

'He looked pretty shaken himself.'

'I am sure they will find another stewardess if you cannot fly,' Farzana said, and Clemency saw that they all expected her to cry off. She must look worse even than she felt.

'I'll be fine.'

In a way, she was more than fine. If today were the day that Petrov made his move, she'd be ready for him.

*

Clemency went into the terminal building to collect the flight manifest and loading sheets. Already some of the passengers were waiting by the departure gate for the flight to be called. As she turned to go, she ran into a man hurrying towards her. He held her, stopped her from falling, and she looked up into his face.

Gemal.

She tried to back away, but he seized her wrist. She was about to break free, to cry out for help, when something in his eyes stopped her. There was no madness, no rage. Only grief.

'Please,' he said in a low, urgent voice. 'Miss Green. Caroline.'

As he spoke, he dipped his head, as if in submission, knowing she had every right to be scared of him. He let his hands drop.

'Please, may we talk? It is only for one moment.'

Around her, the life of the airport was carrying on. Passengers buying duty-free, strolling around, turning the pages of their newspapers and magazines.

'I have to go back to my flight.'

'Please. I wish to say…'

He looked away, as if he were interested in the planes standing on the concrete beyond the windows of the concourse. He looked ill, his eyes sore and ringed with shadows.

'I am so sorry for your friend. She was so lovely, so…' He broke off with a meaningless wave of his hand. 'She was my friend. And that night, also my guest. I cannot be easy until she is… is avenged.'

The word brought an echo of ancient blood feuds and family honour into the sleek, modern airport concourse.

'I have spoken to Colonel Auer,' he went on. 'He thinks you may be able to help.'

'Me?' Her surprise was genuine.

'He said you were perhaps an investigator. Perhaps from your famous Scotland Yard.'

'Of course not.'

'Often, there is a crime, a victim, and the police know who is guilty. But they want evidence. So their hands are tied. But me, I am free. If I know who is the guilty one, then I can act.'

'I don't know anything.'

'I know you must say this. But please, believe me. If you find the name of the one who did this to her, you need only tell me. I will arrange everything.'

He spoke with complete assurance, and she saw now how changed he was. Or perhaps, the inner strength of the man was showing. This was no idle threat, a cry of pain turned to brave words. She was convinced that he would know who to ask, would pay whatever fee was necessary, and Felicity's killer would himself be killed.

For a moment, it seemed so simple. She only had to give him the name. It was as if Petrov himself was sprawled helpless at her feet, and she had a gun in her hand, and there were no witnesses. The perfect crime, except it would be no crime, only justice. For Felicity, and for the all the others who had died at Petrov's hands.

She felt herself flush, her head a little woozy, on the edge of fainting.

'I…'

Then the moment was passed.

'I have to go.'

She turned and hurried away, before temptation became too strong.

*

There was trouble with the inner port engine before take-off and they landed almost an hour late in Ahmar. Clemency went to the Red Air office to pick up the passenger list, only to find Major Hereward looking through the Venetian blinds at the plane, tapping his swagger stick impatiently against his leg. At first she assumed it was something to do with Felicity's murder, but he was much too cheerful.

'Ah, Miss Green. All well? Good. We have some progress.'

It was much more than that. With ill-suppressed excitement, he told her that the plot was unravelling. The Residency had learned that two hijackers were to board the flight. A landing strip had been prepared in the desert, where the plane would be forced down so the Emir and his family could be spirited away.

'The two men are travelling on Egyptian passports. They're posing as engineers. What I want you to do is this.'

He rattled off his instructions, and Clemency frowned as she tried to take it all in. But within a few minutes she was by the door in the departure area, clipboard in hand, and calling out for the passengers for Beirut to come forward ready for boarding. She could see the Emir's party climbing the steps, the fuel truck driving away, Stannard's crates of fruit going into the cargo hold; everything normal. She began to tick off the passengers and let them through.

Glancing down the queue, she saw two men who were so obviously the Egyptian engineers that she wondered why Hereward was bothering with this play-acting of letting them go through to the plane.

They reached the front of the queue and the taller of the men handed over his passport. She flicked through it and checked the name against the list, drawing it out so that the previous passengers would have time to reach the plane. Then she let the passport fall to the floor. She picked it up, handed it to him with a smile and an apology. He waited by the door while she dealt with his colleague, and then they both walked out of the terminal towards the plane, a hundred yards away.

The next passenger moved up. Clemency remembered him from before, Al-Salaam, the cleric who had flown with Suleiman. Disloyally, Clemency hoped he would be sitting in one of Farzana's seats this time.

Her instructions were to delay the next passengers until Hereward's men had done their work. She scanned the list again while the man hissed with impatience.

'What is this delay? Surely you know who I am.'

From the corner of her eye, she watched the two Egyptians. They were halfway across the tarmac to the plane when, quite quietly, two men in uniform came over to them. After a moment, the four of them walked away towards the administration block.

She finished pretending to check Al-Salaam's passport and handed it back to him.

'This treatment is intolerable,' he hissed.

'I am sorry, *Hadrat* Al-Salaam. I—'

But he had swept past her and was striding towards the plane. The two Egyptians were out of sight. It was over. But she felt no relief, no elation; only a strange flatness.

'Are you all right, miss?'

It was the next passenger, peering at her in concern. She produced a smile and began to usher the rest of them through to the plane. Sitting in seat 1A, the Emir would have seen the arrest, the proof that the threat to him had been real; and noted how it was done with such discretion. No wonder Hereward looked so pleased when he appeared at the door of the plane a few minutes later to wish the Emir a pleasant flight. In his cautious way, the Emir too looked satisfied.

As the plane climbed out over the Gulf, then turned towards Beirut, Clemency realised that this would be her last flight; the last time she would be taking orders for lunch, fetching magazines or reassuring anxious flyers. Even the boisterous demands for more drinks from the back row, or Al-Salaam clicking his fingers for her to attend to him, could not spoil the moment.

It was over, except for the one thing she had come for: Petrov. If he was in Ahmar, then surely Hereward would sweep him up with the rest of the conspirators. It was more likely that he would be at the desert rendezvous, and she wished she'd asked Hereward if they knew where that was. Busy as she was, she was impatient for the flight to be over, so she could learn what had happened. If they had Petrov, then at last there would be a card of sufficient value to exchange for Peter.

She dared not hope; she couldn't help herself.

Now Al-Salaam, the man who had been so rude to her in the queue, was standing in the aisle, gesturing to her.

'You! Come and see this. It is disgusting!'

As she approached, he grabbed her arm and pulled her to the door of the toilet.

She looked inside. It was exactly as she had left it when she had checked it a few minutes before.

Then she felt something cold and hard pressing into her spine. His voice was quiet in her ear.

'Do not make a sound, or I will kill you.'

# 23

Clemency sat in seat 3C, her eyes to the floor, as she'd been told. Farzana was in the next seat, doing the same, except that her lips were moving soundlessly as she prayed. One of the men from the back of the plane was watching over them from the doorway to the cockpit, and she knew that the other was at the far end, by the galley, doing the same. Each had a gun in his hand.

Had there been a moment she could have stopped them? Perhaps. But her courage had failed her.

She kept reliving the moment: his face close to her ear, his breath hot on her neck. She had managed to get out the words she had rehearsed, how firing a gun would blow a hole in the fragile skin of the plane and would kill them all.

Al-Salaam had just snorted, and said she was stupid and ill-informed, and that in any case his gun had bullets adapted to break up on impact.

'They will not pass through your body,' he had said. 'Instead, they will blow your back to pieces.'

He'd said it as if he'd enjoy pulling the trigger. And she had known that she would do anything in the world to stop that happening. He had manoeuvred her to the cockpit door and told her to open it; and she had done so. Stannard had turned, taken in the scene: Clemency's stricken face, the man smiling coldly behind her, and then turning the gun to point at Stannard's heart.

That was another time she could have fought back.

A twist in his arms, a downward blow to his hand, and perhaps it would all have been over before it began. Instead, he had sent her sprawling, and stepped into the cockpit, forcing Stannard back into his seat.

That would have been the time the two men at the back of the plane had come forward with their guns at the ready to neutralise the Emir's bodyguard.

The one facing backwards had realised something was wrong and had risen to his feet, but as soon as he drew his dagger and advanced towards the men, one of them had shot him in the knee. The other, though, had still turned and leapt from his seat and charged them, his knife against the other man's gun. He had twenty feet to cover and was dead before taking three paces.

The middle rows of the cabin were like an abattoir, with blood over the seats, the floor, and the passengers. The bodyguard had been shot in the chest, and as Al-Salaam had promised, the bullets were adapted to explode on impact. The whole front of his body was a mass of flesh and bone, and his face, splattered with blood, wore an expression of the utmost surprise.

The other was barely conscious, probably bleeding to death; even Fatima, with all her medical training, could not stem the flow of blood from his ruined leg.

All the passengers were told to stay in their seats with their heads bent to their knees. All had obeyed. In place of the cries and screams during the brief fight, they were quiet, except for a woman who was sobbing to herself. The man had died beside her, and her robes were bright with his blood, and she had screamed until one of the men had struck her hard across the face.

The only one free to move about was Fatima, who had fetched a towel for the injured man; and then some cords to make a tourniquet. Now she spoke in Arabic to the guard by the door and he shrugged, then opened the door to the cockpit. After a few words, he exchanged places with Al-Salaam.

'What is it?' he asked impatiently.

'This man must reach a hospital soon,' Fatima said. 'He has lost a lot of blood.'

'You are a doctor. You look after him.'

'I can do nothing. He needs blood. If not, he will die and that will be on your conscience.'

But Al-Salaam just laughed.

'You do not understand. If I have to kill you all, I will do that, and I will not think of it again. You, all of you, are worth nothing.'

'That's not how I see it.'

Al-Salaam swung round. Macquarie was standing in the cockpit doorway. He looked sick, his face grey, and Clemency realised with a shock that it wasn't only the strain of the hijack: he was a seriously ill man. But he still had the spirit to challenge Al-Salaam.

'These are my passengers. My responsibility. I'll co-operate, but not at the cost of a man's life. If he needs a hospital, we'll just have to fly him to the nearest one, and that's that.'

Al Salaam seemed to shrink. For a moment, Clemency thought that maybe Macquarie had found the answer; that his decency and honesty, his moral authority, might seize the initiative from the hijackers.

'The nearest town is Amman,' he went on. 'We'll land there, put him off, maybe some of the other passengers, if you're happy with that. Then we'll take off again and fly you to wherever you want to go. I'll plot the course now.'

Al-Salaam stood still, his face crimson with rage. He swallowed convulsively. Macquarie turned to go back into the cockpit. Without another word, the other man dragged out his gun and shot him in the back.

Her ears were deafened by the shot; her nose wrinkled at the acrid smoke; and Macquarie had fallen almost at her feet; yet Clemency could not believe it. She stared at the cruel wound in his back.

Though his eyes were open, he didn't seem to be in pain. Without thinking, she crouched down and took his hand, then looked around. Fatima made to come forward, but Al-Salaam gestured to her to keep back. Maybe it didn't matter. Macquarie was beyond any help. Clemency took a deep breath, trying not to weep, and laid her hand on his broad shoulder. His eyes turned to her, and for a moment she thought he might try and speak. There was blood flowing from his mouth, and he coughed a couple of times. His breath stopped, and his eyes went very thoughtful, and then he was dead.

She looked up. Stannard was there, his skin greenish and his hand to his mouth; Farzana, her eyes swimming with tears; Fatima, showing nothing behind the doctor's mask; Khalid, his eyes wide in shock. Al-Salaam was staring down at her. In his fury he could have shot her too. Instead, he pulled her away impatiently and threw her back into her seat. Then he pushed his gun into Stannard's stomach and forced him back into the cockpit.

Next to her, Farzana was saying a prayer in Farsi; her voice low, so as not to draw the attention of the guards. Then she switched to English, but still in the same tone.

'Don't do anything. Not yet. Don't throw your life away.'

She had sensed that Clemency was on the edge of

madness; or turning her shock in violent action. So Fatima was doing what she could to calm her.

'Do nothing. For him. For me.'

Clemency nodded.

Time passed; then the plane banked to port, a slow turn that would take them south-west. So at least that part of Hereward's information had been right: it would be a desert landing. The rest? How easy it had been for the conspirators to distract Hereward with the supposedly-suspicious Egyptians. She pictured them watching the British with more subtlety, and probably with better sources of information; and understanding that anything that looked like the work of Nassar would be seized on by the Residency.

It had worked. With his nervous bullying, Al-Salaam might have aroused her suspicions. So might the two mute Arabs who had come on board last, clutching their hand luggage. Or maybe she would have thought they were merely first-time flyers; and that Al-Salaam merely hated Western women, and she would have let them board anyway. Either way, Bill Macquarie was dead; and the Emir would follow him; and maybe Fatima and Khalid too, and the rest of his entourage.

There was nothing she could do.

Al-Salaam had his pistol, and the two others each had some kind of machine gun. He had posted them by the cockpit door, commanding the whole length of the cabin. Anyone standing could be cut down in an instant.

Clemency felt Farzana's knee rest against hers, as if in comfort. Then she realised there was some other meaning in her gesture. She looked carefully to her side, and Farzana directed her gaze to the floor.

It was one of the long daggers that the bodyguards had held, dropped and forgotten when they were shot. During the last few minutes, Farzana had managed to reach out with her foot and draw it to her. She wanted Clemency to take it. Why? Because she was scared to use it herself? No, it would be because Clemency was in the aisle seat and would have the best opportunity.

Slowly, carefully, she drew it closer, then reached down between her legs and lifted it up. It was surprisingly heavy, and the blade was wickedly sharp. If you could get close enough, it would go through flesh like butter. She dropped it into the pouch in the front of her tabard, where it lay heavily.

Now the shame of her capitulation to Al-Salaam began to ebb. In its place came a cold anger and a desire to kill the man who had planned this evil, who had shot the guards, who had murdered Macquarie because he recognised a man of greater courage and integrity than his own.

Al-Salaam now went to the intercom by the cabin door and lifted the handset.

'Ladies and gentlemen.'

His voice was calm, arrogant, and caught their attention.

'My name is El-Mutahir. I am now the commander of this aeroplane.'

*Mutahir.* It had come up in one of her Arabic lessons: something to do with purifying.

'Unfortunately,' he went on, savouring the moment, 'some fools have tried to defy me. The same will happen to you unless you do exactly as I say.

'My instructions are these. You must stay in your seat at all times with your head on your knees. You must not talk. You must not signal. You must not stand up or try to move. Anyone who disobeys me will be killed.'

He looked up and down the cabin and saw no-one trying to challenge him. Pleased, he allowed himself a brief smile.

'You will want to know what is to happen next. I will tell you. This plane under my command will soon land. Those who are worthy in the eyes of Allah, the all-seeing, the all-knowing, will be allowed to leave the plane. But there are others who have defied the will of Allah, and they will stay on the plane, and we will leave to go to another place with them.'

Clemency was trying to understand this twist when the plane turned abruptly and began to descend. She saw an expanse of desert, flat and empty, and the engines were throttled back and the flaps began to extend. A rough airstrip, Hereward had said.

Realising the risk, Farzana raised her hands high and stood up, explaining to Al-Salaam that she must prepare the passengers. He was angry, but he saw the sense in it. Farzana called out to the passengers to put on their seatbelts as hard as they could, remove sharp objects, glasses and shoes, and brace themselves.

She was still standing when the wheels touched the ground.

It was a beautiful landing, perfectly level. Except for the clatter of stones being thrown up against the rear of the fuselage, it might have been the runway at Beirut. Clemency thought of Stannard alone in the cockpit, save for the man with a gun pointing at him. She might not like him or trust him, but as Macquarie had said, he was a damn good pilot.

# 24

Once the plane had slowed to a halt, the younger of the two guards, hardly more than a boy, pulled Clemency roughly from her seat and dragged her down the aisle to open the rear door. The heat outside, and the dust thrown up by the engines blowing in, made her flinch. But already they were hurrying the passengers out of their seats and she hardly had time to help them drop the few feet to the ground. Then she was pushed out herself.

She picked herself up and looked about. The passengers were standing in a group, covered by a guard with a machine gun. For a few minutes nothing happened and she looked back along the line they had taken on landing, and her respect for Stannard rose. There was no trace of a landing strip: it was just flat desert. He must have had nerves of steel to put the plane down with a gun at his back, having seen what they had done to Macquarie.

Or perhaps he had been bribed after all, and had been prepared for the challenge.

'Ladies and gentlemen.' Al-Salaam had appeared in the doorway above them. 'This will be your new home until you are rescued. There is a hut with water and food. Enough for several days. The authorities will be informed of your position.'

He turned and went back inside. The guards hurried them all to their feet, past the end of the wing. There were two Land Rovers standing about fifty yards away, and more guards with rifles, and next to them, two men; one was an Arab in a dark suit and tie and sporting a Panama hat; the other was a Westerner. In his khaki shirt and shorts and wearing dark glasses, Petrov looked at home in the desert.

He turned to watch them approach.

The passengers kept walking, and Clemency with them. They were being taken towards a hut further down the strip, half-derelict, dark against the blinding light. As they passed by, Petrov's eyes swept over the crowd of passengers. Then his gaze returned to settle on her. He leaned down and spoke in Russian to the man at his side. She couldn't hear the words. But the man called out in Arabic.

'Not the stewardess.'

She pretended not to understand. Only when one of the guards came towards her and put the barrel of his rifle against her stomach did she stop. The rest of the passengers passed around her and carried on. No-one looked back to see her fate.

She couldn't look at Petrov. Would he order the man to fire? Or did he have other plans? Torture, to see if she knew anything? Or simply for revenge?

She closed her eyes. All she could do was live in this moment. The sand shifting beneath her thin shoes. The faint breeze rustling the fabric of her tunic. The sun harsh on her face. Her breath coming slowly, carefully, as she struggled to stay calm.

Then the voice again.

'Put her back on the plane.'

The man jabbed her in the stomach and she came out of her trance. She stumbled back, and turned towards the plane, and the barrel prodded her along.

Perhaps it made a kind of sense. There were to be no witnesses; no loose ends. Petrov did not want to bother with her. Putting her on the plane was a death sentence, to be enacted away from the other passengers.

She came to the open door and pulled herself on board, wincing because the steel of the frame was already burning hot in the sun. The older guard was standing there but made no effort to help. She closed and locked the door, then made her way down the empty cabin.

Now it was just the five of them; Farzana beside her, showing both sympathy and relief that Clemency had not been left behind after all; Fatima across the aisle, outwardly calm, except when her eyes flicked to her son at her side; Khalid tense, studying everything; Hamid, the Emir's secretary, with a tic in his cheek and fear in his eyes; and the Emir, the fulcrum of all this, his face drawn with the pain of his illness, but his eyes still burning.

*He knows,* Clemency thought; *he knows that one of his sons has done this; and he knows which one.*

The plane's engines had been running all this time, and already they were moving, passing the hut and the group of passengers outside it, then turning to line up on the runway again. They had been on the ground less than five minutes. Al-Salaam had not wasted time in needless discussion with Petrov; and that meant it was all going exactly to plan.

They rose away from the airstrip and then turned to the east, or a little to the south of east, a heading that would take them back towards Ahmar and the Persian Gulf. But they were also climbing as quickly as they could, the engines straining, so that Clemency's ears were popping with the abrupt change in pressure. Soon they would be out of sight of the passengers below, and free to choose whatever heading they wished.

Why had Petrov not spoken to her? He must have known she was on the plane. She had thought of the mission as a duel between the two of them, with Peter as the prize. But that was just a delusion. She simply didn't matter to him. Even in that strange setting, in the middle of the desert, he had been so cool, so much in control. Perhaps it was odd that he could not speak the language, just like the British or Americans or French. But then, the Soviet union was just another empire. Instead of cricket and scotch, or freedom and bourbon, it brought class struggle and vodka. But it wanted the same. Air bases. Naval facilities. Oil.

She was sick of it all. What was she about to die for? Ahmar? England? Or the directors and shareholders of British Petroleum?

Farzana nudged her; then began to talk as quietly as she could, her voice masked by the engines, so Clemency had to strain to make out the message; but the gist was clear. While she was on the ground, they had agreed on a plan. When the time came, it was for Clemency to deal with the guard standing in the aisle just behind her. She wondered who had come up with it and whether they had any idea what they were doing: but there was no alternative. It would have to work, or they would all soon be dead.

They ran into a patch of turbulence, the plane bouncing in the columns of hot air rising from the desert. The young guard beside Clemency half-fell and steadied himself against the back of her seat. Hamid began to moan. Clemency felt Farzana's foot pressed onto hers. She reached for the handle of the knife.

The bucketing continued. Hamid stood up, one hand to his mouth, the other gesturing to show he was going to be sick. He stumbled towards the door of the toilet.

'Stop!' the older guard said. He stepped forward, the gun swinging round, as Fatima rose from her seat and snatched the fire extinguisher from its bracket on the front bulkhead.

But she had left it a second too late. The guard pulled up his machine gun and fired.

The bullets caught Hamid, spun him around, a line of red holes across his white shirt.

At once there was a blast from the cockpit, a hurricane of air mixed with dust, cushions, paper cups, magazines. The guard put up his arm to shield his eyes, just as Fatima smashed the fire extinguisher down on the back of his head.

The younger guard at Clemency's side had ducked too, almost into her lap. She drove the knife up into his ribs, ignoring the grotesque sensation as the blade ripped through skin and muscle. He cried out, fell backwards, and Clemency slipped from her seat as if to help him. She found the handle of the knife beneath the man's robes and drove it twice more into his heart.

The cabin had filled with a thick mist, the sign of an explosive depressurisation. One of the bullets fired at Hamid must have broken a window. Then, over the deafening roar of the air, she heard another shot. She crawled down the aisle to the shelter of the galley, gasping in the thin air. Darkness was already creeping into her vision and she reached up for the emergency bottle of oxygen. She clamped the mask to her face and turned the wheel to let the gas flow, then took a deep breath.

In a few moments her head had cleared. She risked

a quick look around the galley bulkhead and took in the scene.

Fatima was standing over her father, holding an oxygen mask to his face. Khalid was staring at the body of one of the guards. And Farzana was struggling against the flow of air, as if wading up a fast-flowing stream, towards the cockpit.

There was no-one else in sight; no-one else alive.

Farzana's movements were strangely slow. She leaned against the side of the cabin, one hand to her throat, and then slowly slid to the floor.

Fatima looked over to where she lay. But then her eyes rolled up into her head and she too pitched forward.

Clemency was already battling her way down the aisle, grasping the seat backs like rungs of a ladder. She passed the other hijacker, lying dead or unconscious over two of the seats; and then the body of Al-Salaam. There was a neat hole in his forehead, and his eyes stared blankly towards the cabin ceiling.

She reached the two women. Instinct told her to use her own mask to revive them, but the rule was to help yourself before helping anyone else. If she were to pass out, then they would all die. She shook her head to banish the confusion. That wasn't right. Stannard would make an emergency descent and they would soon be able to breathe once more.

It was routine; Farzana had explained it. It would be like plunging down in a lift, frightening but quite safe. Within a minute or so, the air would be breathable once more.

But they were still flying straight and level.

She kneeled beside Fatima and gestured to Khalid to join her. She mimed to him to use the mask to revive his mother, then himself, and then his father again. He nodded and put down gun clenched in his hand. His eyes were filled with shock and she guessed he was the one who had killed Al Salaam. But there was no time to worry about that. She stumbled forward to the cockpit.

The front right windscreen was completely gone, and the noise and the blast of air was like nothing she could have imagined. Everything that was loose – belts, maps, cables – was flapping and flailing viciously, while the stream of air beat against her, so that even crawling forward, holding onto the frame of the seats for support, took an age.

Only once she was in the comparative shelter of the captain's seat did she realise what was missing.

The cockpit was empty.

Her gaze turned to the space where the windscreen had been. There were no fragments of glass on Stannard's seat. The pressure must have blown outwards like a bomb. And Mike Stannard had gone with it.

# 25

She stared at the void, the blue beyond, a distant line of clouds, and her mind struggled past the horror of his death to its consequences. There was no-one alive on board the plane who could fly.

For now, the autopilot ensured that the plane continued on its plotted course. It would do so until they ran out of fuel and began to fall towards the earth.

She climbed into the captain's seat. The microphone for the radio was in its usual place, but the radio itself had been wrecked by the hijackers. The front was torn from the panel, leaving a mass of wires hanging down. There was no way to contact the ground for advice or assistance.

She forced herself to think. The plane would fly for at least another three hours. But by then the passengers would all be dead. She had to get the plane down to an altitude where they could breathe.

Macquarie had talked about the autopilot. He'd gestured to it. And here it was, on the control panel in front of her. There was a knob, and it was set to 27. She found the altimeter, and it read 27,000 feet.

She hesitated, then clicked the knob of the autopilot round to 26.

The throttle levers to her right slid back, and over the storm-blast of the air through the shattered windscreen she could imagine the engine noise easing a little.

There was a sensation of sinking. Her stomach

lurched, but it wasn't only fear; the plane was starting to descend.

The altimeter began to unwind, gently showing their descent. Soon they were at 26,000 feet. The throttles inched forward in that uncanny way, as if invisible hands were at the controls, and the plane settled down to flying at the new height.

She repeated the operation. 25. 24. 23. For a moment, she was back at school, in a geography lesson. *The height of Mount Everest is 29,029 feet.* They were already below that. Soon the air would be breathable.

The plane continued to sink, the control column and throttles to move, and she left elated at the idea that this massive and complex machine was responding to her commands.

Farzana came in, standing behind her to keep out of the blast through the broken windscreen.

'How are they?' Clemency shouted out.

'They will live. What about Mr Stannard?'

'He's dead.' She sensed Farzana looking around; her puzzlement. 'He must have gone through the window.'

'What do we do?' Farzana's voice rose in fear.

Clemency had no answer. The hundreds of dials and switches and levers mocked her. Somewhere in their complexity was the answer of how to land the plane safely, but she could not read their language. The ones she understood were no help. They were at 15,000 feet, heading 315 and at 330 knots. But how much time did they have? How much fuel? When would they need to turn towards the airport? And what would happen if she disconnected the autopilot and held the controls herself?

Clemency looked out of the side window at the desert passing so far below. It was quite beautiful in the afternoon sun, and tears came to her eyes. She didn't want to die.

There was no-one else to ask; no-one to turn to. Macquarie was dead. Stannard was dead. No-one else knew any more than she did about the operation of the plane. The responsibility was hers, and hers alone.

Alone. Something Macquarie had said about the captain's seat. Responsibility. Now she was sitting in the seat, and it had fallen to her to save the others.

'Farzana, I need you to help with the checklists. Somewhere there is a book, a kind of ring-bound folder, with the instructions for landing. Read it and tell me what I need to know.'

Clemency began to think it through. The dial on the autopilot allowed her to make the plane go up and down, and there was a similar dial for the heading. But she had no idea where they were, so couldn't work out which direction to go. She might take them deeper into the desert or towards the mountains or over the sea.

Perhaps it would be better to put down in the desert, if it were flat enough. She could simply instruct the plane to fly lower and lower, and then ease back the power, and it would settle onto the ground. The plane would be wrecked, but they would have some chance of surviving.

'I can't find the folder,' Farzana said. 'I think it must have blown away.'

'OK.'

'Have you called the ground? The air traffic control?'

'No. The radio's smashed.'

Farzana was muttering under her breath in Persian.

'We'll be OK. I can land this plane.'

Farzana looked incredulous, her eyes wide.

'You?'

If Farzana didn't believe in her, they were finished. Trying to be calm, she leaned forward and flicked off the auto-pilot and took the controls in her hands. Then, as she had practised with Macquarie, she banked the plane very slightly to the right. The mountains that had filled the horizon began to slide slowly away to port. She brought the plane onto the new course, reset the auto-pilot to continue the descent and reengaged it.

'The desert here is flat. We can land. But you'll need to get them strapped in and then come back and help me. I can't reset the autopilot and work all the other stuff.'

The plane flew on, still descending. It was featureless below, like the salt pans of Ahmar. In the far distance there were hills, and to the left some higher, sharper peaks. The sooner they were down, the better. They were passing through seven thousand feet.

Farzana returned from the cabin with a thick scarf that she wrapped around her head and shoulders so that only her eyes showed, sheltering her from the air blasting through the shattered windscreen.

'There's a wheel to your right. It's got some numbers on it. Five, ten, fifteen and so on. If I ask for flaps ten or flaps fifteen, you just turn the wheel. OK?'

'Sure.' Farzana had caught some of Clemency's mood.

'In front of you there's a dial with the air speed on. It should be reading about 240 knots. Can you keep shouting that out as we come into land, so we don't let the speed drop too much?'

'OK. What speed should it be?'

Clemency wasn't sure. It was another thing that was in the missing handbook. What had Macquarie said? 120 knots? They would find out quickly enough if she were wrong and the plane stalled.

'The dial to the right is the height. Can you call that out as well? I want to be looking forward.'

The ground was coming closer. It was possible to make out the texture of the desert, different colours in the sand and gravel, the occasional skeleton of a thorn bush. Still it was beautifully flat. Or looked that way.

They passed a thousand feet.

'Can you see anything that looks like the wheels?'

'Yes, that's right here,' Farzana said. 'Shall I do that now?'

There came the familiar rumble as the wheels deployed, and the reassuring clunk as they locked into place. They felt the drag slowing them down.

'Turn the flaps wheel round to 10.'

Farzana began calling out the height and the speed.

'Four hundred feet. A hundred and forty speed.'

They were sinking again. But Clemency was absorbed by the throb of the engines through the control column, through the floor. In the sound of the engines, she could imagine she could hear music.

'A hundred feet.'

She laid her hands on the control column and leaned forward to turn off the autopilot. There was no immediate change in the whine of the engines, the mass of meaningless dials and gauges in front and above her, or in the view through the windscreen. She moved the column slowly back, and the plane responded, just as it had when Macquarie had been alive and at her side.

The flatlands fell away as the nose rose to the sky. The altimeter wound itself backwards like a clock in a cartoon; thirty feet... twenty feet...

The plane touched and bounced a little into the air again. She'd forgotten to ease back on the power. One wing dipped and she waited for it to dig into the ground and flip the plane into a crash. Then the plane steadied. Unable to look away from the horizon, her hand felt across the controls until she had the throttles and was ready to pull them back.

They sank, touched again, and she cut the engines and this time they held. The noise was appalling, the vibration shaking the whole plane until it was certain it must fall apart. The instruments were a blur, every loose item in the cockpit had flown from its place. As their speed came away, the nose sank down and the nosewheel hit the ground, jarring, and it was a miracle it didn't collapse.

And still they rolled on.

There was some way of reversing the thrust of the engines, but Clemency couldn't remember. She had lost the initiative, and was now a helpless passenger on this runaway vehicle rolling across the desert.

But they were slowing. She was leaning on the straps as the speed fell away.

Each thud was more of a separate event. No longer like driving at speed over cobbles, magnified a hundred times.

The plane slewed round a little. Had it happened earlier, they would have tipped over; now it didn't seem to mean very much. Everything looked the same in every direction.

They had stopped.

They sat for a long time, until the whine of the engines brought them back to reality. Farzana unwound the scarf from her face and began to study the controls at her side, and then over her head. After a moment she reached up and flicked a switch, then looked out of the side window. One of the blurs of the propeller was slowing, until it became four slashing scimitars, and then a windmill, and was finally slowing to a halt.

Satisfied, she flipped the three switches beside it, and the pitch of the engines began to fall, and a moment after they were sitting in a strange world of silence.

Clemency could not move; except that her right hand was shaking. But Farzana was unlocking her belt, helping her to her feet.

'You did well,' she said.

Clemency remembered that Bill Macquarie was lying dead in the cabin.

'I had a good teacher.'

# 26

They buried the bodies a little way away from the plane, in the shade of a stunted thorn tree, wrapped in red airline blankets. They had nothing with which to dig into the sandy soil, so they piled small stones on each one. They still hoped it was temporary; that in a day, two at most, the plane would be found.

Khalid helped them, but Fatima stayed with the Emir. He was much worse, his breathing laboured, and she explained that he's had some kind of seizure during the descent.

'Will he be all right?' Clemency had asked anxiously. It wasn't that she cared particularly for him, or was worried about the politics of Ahmar. But she had taken on Macquarie's responsibility for the safety of the passengers, and she hated the idea that the conspirators might win after all, should the Emir die before the succession was secure. But they helped him down the stairs, and the open air and the surrounding desert revived him a little. He sat very still, conserving his strength, as his daughter explained what had happened and where they were.

That done, Clemency and Farzana went through the plane, working out what supplies they had, in case they had to stay there a long time. But then Fatima called them over.

'My father wished to say to you that he is grateful to you. You helped to save his life and that of his family.'

He looked so serious that Clemency had to find something equally formal to say in return. She didn't risk her Arabic, but instead asked Fatima to thank the Emir and explain that as the crew of the plane, their duty was to safeguard their passengers. But it seemed this wasn't his meaning; Fatima explained that it was their defeat of the hijackers.

Clemency hadn't wanted to be reminded of the man – the boy – she had killed. Carrying him out to be buried along with the others had put ice in her heart. But somehow the Emir had retrieved the two knives that had belonged to his bodyguards; and he now presented one to Clemency and the other to Farzana, with a speech that praised their courage and loyalty.

She took the knife with mixed emotions. Expected to respond, she said that she was serving her own sovereign who had commanded her to protect the Emir. He looked pleased, though Clemency wondered what Farzana would think. For that was one thing that had fallen into place as she had collected the stones to mark the graves. She was sure now – had in some way known for a long time – that Farzana was no more a stewardess than she was herself. She too was serving a reigning monarch: but in Farzana's case, it was the Shah of Iran.

*

The sun was setting. They built a fire a little way away from the plane, and Farzana and Clemency agreed they would take turns to keep it burning all night, in the hope that it would be spotted from the air; Fatima would stay in the shelter of the cabin with the Emir and Khalid, who had been persuaded that they had plenty of food for now, and there was no need to go off to hunt.

There was no shortage of fuel, either; the plane still held hundreds of gallons of aviation spirit, and after some trial and error they found a way to drain it from one of the wing tanks, and Khalid showed them how to soak a metal box of sand with fuel so that would burn for half an hour or more.

'There's almost twenty gallons of water in the galley tank,' Farzana said, returning from the plane with pans, cups and a box of tea. 'And there are the bottled drinks. If we're careful, they should last for a week or more.'

'They'll come before that, won't they? We must have been reported missing hours ago.'

'We were off our course for so long. That will mean they will be looking in the wrong place.'

But Farzana didn't seem worried, as if the simple camp chores were reassuring.

'Did you ever live in the desert?' Clemency asked. 'You seem at home here.'

'No, but I would go often with my family to the mountains. Riding and hunting. My home town is called Aleshtar. It is very dry. Though not like this.'

They prepared some food and took it to the Emir and Fatima in the cabin, then came back to look after the fire. By now it was dark, the stars unbelievably clear in the night sky. They sipped their tea, and it was so like the night they had spent on the plane in Ahmar that Clemency believed she could break through the shell of reserve that Farzana always had wrapped around her.

She threw some more wood onto the fire.

'I suppose,' she began, 'if I were the Iranian secret

service, I'd be very interested in an airline that served the Persian Gulf. Who was coming or going. Passenger lists, passport numbers, visas.'

Farzana wrapped her cloak closer around her. For a moment, Clemency thought she was going to deny it; but as so often, Farzana's thinking had run quickly ahead.

'It was something else. Let me show you.'

Puzzled, Clemency followed her to the nose of the plane and the hatch for the forward cargo hold. Farzana dragged out one of the crates and prised off the thin wooden lid.

'We should use this for the fire,' she said in passing. 'But that is not important. This is what I came for.'

She took out a string bag filled with coconuts and carried it back to the fire. She took one out, examined it minutely as best she could in the flickering firelight, then rested it on the sand, digging it in slightly so it would not move. Then she took the knife – more like a machete – that the Emir had presented to her and brought it down on the coconut, splitting it neatly in two.

Clemency had expected a splash of milk. Instead, the halves fell apart with the interior seemingly completely filled with the white meat of the coconut. But when she reached out, it crumbled into pieces. She sniffed the powder on her finger and was about to lick it when Farzana stopped her.

'I would not do that. It is pure heroin.'

'Oh. Well, I wouldn't know what it tasted like anyway.'

'We have been looking for the channel for drugs for a year. We knew it was coming from Iran by *dhow* to Ahmar, and that the weekly flight was the most likely way for it to be passed on to Europe.'

'So it was Stannard?'

'Yes, working for Rossiter.'

'Rossiter?'

Farzana looked almost disappointed in Clemency.

'Of course. Taking the drugs to Beirut was not enough. It was the chance to fly it to Cyprus, and from there to your military bases in England, not to the airports where the customs might ask questions. Ahmar to Beirut, Beirut to Nicosia, and Nicosia to England. To an airfield called, I think, Brize Norton.'

In Farzana's lightly accented English, it sounded as exotic as any Arab or Persian village.

'So Rossiter had to know?'

'It was his idea. His airline was in difficulties two years ago and he looked for more investment from businessmen in the region. The money arrived, but there were strings attached.'

'And he recruited Stannard?'

'Stannard was already working for Red Air. When he was at BOAC there was some trouble and he had to leave. Rossiter liked to employ pilots who could not easily find work elsewhere. Like Captain Macquarie.'

'He didn't know, did he?'

'Of course not. For him, it was his health. That is why he flew with Red Air. He would not have passed the medical of another airline, but Rossiter arranged for him to visit a friendly doctor in Beirut who provided the necessary certificate. In this way, Captain Macquarie could keep flying.'

'What was wrong?'

'Cancer. I do not think he would have lived much longer.'

'So he knew that when he was showing me how to fly.'

'And it was a pleasure to him as well. But yes, I think he felt guilty for wanting to keep flying as long as he could. I told him he was a good pilot and the passengers were safe with him, but still it troubled him. He was planning to give up in a few weeks. If he lived that long. And so he helped us to be heroes.'

'Heroines. A female hero is a heroine.'

'If you wish. But we landed the plane. The newspapers will want to know everything, will they not? They will want our photographs. Perhaps even on television.'

'Oh.'

'Yes. It would be very bad for us both. But I have an idea. Captain Macquarie was the hero. He landed the plane. Unfortunately, he then died of his wounds. What do you think?'

Clemency thought of Hall's Creek, the small town in Western Australia that he had spoken of with such fondness; where he had hoped one day he would return. If he could not, at least they could be proud of his end.

'Well, it's true, isn't it? He told us how to do it.'

They fell silent. As the fire died down, the stars became yet brighter. Even in the highlands of Scotland, Clemency had never seen a sky like it. From far off came a strange and chilling screech.

'What do you think that was?' she asked.

'A hyena?'

Clemency was reminded of a question that had been puzzling her since Farzana had shown her the drugs.

'If that's why you were at Red Air, was it just coincidence about the Emir and the hijacking?'

'Yes and no. Our information was that Red Air was part of the scheme, but not which flights or which pilots. When we learned of the plot against the Emir, then I tried to be on as many of those flights as I could. Unfortunately, I could not be there all the time as there was a new crew member that Rossiter wanted to stay on the route.'

'Me?'

'We thought that perhaps you were there for the British secret service. You see, you had not been trained as a stewardess, and the British delight in improvisation.'

'So you're a professional agent? I mean, it's your job?'

'You are surprised? My grandfather was the chief of our clan and my father was his second son. He joined the Army and then the Intelligence. When he died, they wished to do something to help my family, and I became a cadet in his old unit. It is a great honour to serve in this way, to him and to my country.'

'They let women do intelligence work?'

'Our country is changing very quickly. It is only this last year that women could vote. Imagine it. My mother and I, going to the polling station together. She cried. Now it is common for girls to go to university, or have a job. You can go to a party with a boy and no-one thinks you are bad. In my people, the Lur, this is not such a change as women have always had more freedom but for my friends in Teheran, this is not something their parents could ever have done.'

She paused to throw more wood onto the fire.

'Iran is becoming powerful once more. We need to protect ourselves. From the Soviets. Perhaps even from England.'

'I thought we were allies.'

'We are. For now.' There was a cynical note in her voice. 'But we have longer memories than you. My father, he was in the army when the British invaded us. It was a humiliation. A good friend of his died when his ship was destroyed by your navy. We are now allies, but we do not forget. That is why we must be strong. And we need to know the secret plans of other countries. Then, your army and navy attacked without warning. There was no declaration of war. We were caught in our sleep and we lost our country in four days. So we need a strong intelligence to protect us.'

'But why Ahmar?'

'Is Ahmar not on the Persian Gulf? Do we not have the right to know what is happening here? Or do the English think it is theirs until the end of time?'

Farzana's sudden vehemence startled Clemency; but it was gone just as quickly.

'I am sorry. I do not mean to lecture you.'

She poked the fire, sending sparks dancing up in to the night.

'Don't worry,' Clemency said. 'I don't care who runs Ahmar so long as it isn't the Soviets. That's the only reason I'm here.'

'Of course. Your people have been against the Russians for two hundred years.'

'It's not the Russians. It's the Communists.'

'Then I am with you. In my country, the Shah is for reform. He has the money, from oil, but there are many who oppose him. There are clerics who stand to lose from these changes. If you let people decide on the government, then maybe they will want to decide about their spiritual leaders too. If you give people freedoms, they may choose to listen to modern ways, and not the past. The clerics wish to control us. They do not like women going to college, as I did. Or working. Or choosing what we wear or who we marry.

They want everything to be as it was a thousand years ago.

'Of course, they cannot stop this change. But they can cause much trouble. They are now working with the Communists, the Tabur, who are so well-organised, and have people everywhere. They are strange allies, because they agree on nothing except that they want to tear down the Shah, and the freedom we now have.

'But what are the Communists to you? There are no Communists in England.'

Clemency found it hard to explain.

'It's like an evil thing. The way it… it says that ends justify the means. It takes away our humanity. It's not an abstract idea. I've seen what they do. I've stood there and watched them kill innocent people. Shoot them in the back. They torture and take hostages and…'

She stopped and took a deep breath.

'Come, I will make tea,' Farzana said. 'You are not like the English in the Residency. You are more like the English poets I read at school. You have a soul.'

# 27

Clemency awoke just before dawn, stiff and cold. She prodded the embers of the fire with a piece of wood, then rested a pan of water on the hottest part of the ashes, crouching over it, warming herself as best she could. It was odd to think that, in a few hours' time, she'd be trying to find some shade to escape from the heat of the day; but the chill had settled deep.

While the water began to steam, the outline of the plane took shape, and the horizon, and the vastness of the desert, slowly emerging from the shadows behind her. There was a slow movement behind her as Fazana woke up.

'Have you seen anything?' It was Khalid, calling from the door of the cabin.

'There was a plane in the night,' Clemency called back. 'It circled us. I think they saw the fire. How is the Emir?'

'Not so good.'

Clemency said that there would soon be tea; at least that was one thing about having the plane; no shortage of fuel. Though the problem with kerosene was that it burned so purely that there was very little smoke. No good for signalling their presence during the hours of daylight. Perhaps she could use some of the foam from the seats...

From behind, from the darkness of the west, came a metallic sound; familiar, yet impossible to place. She peered into the gloom. There were indistinct shapes on the side of the nearest hill. Then she had it; the clink of a harness.

There were five of them; each on a camel, wrapped in cloaks and with scarves over their faces, padding slowly over the desert in a scene that had changed little in three thousand years. Odd to think that in a world of planes and radio and radar, rescue should come from the back of a dromedary.

She walked forward to meet them.

'Clemency!'

It was Farzana's voice, urgent, warning. But too late.

The nearest of the men had produced a rifle and was pointing it at her. He snapped some words, too fast for her to catch.

'It's all right,' she said in her halting Arabic. 'I'm not one of the hijackers. The Emir is safe.'

The man unwrapped his scarf. It was Suleiman.

'Don't kill her yet. I have questions for her.'

With this, he kicked the camel into life and rode past her, towards the plane.

*

They had called the desert a sea; and how easy it would be to take them away, and bury them in one of the shifting dunes, with no more chance of being found than if they were weighed down and dropped into the deepest part of the ocean. Faced with this, Clemency found refuge in piecing together how this had happened. The plane they had heard had been sent by the rebels. The pilot had signalled to Suleiman, who had then travelled through the night. He had watched from the hills, and realised that his plan had misfired.

Now it was time for the ritual exchanges. Suleiman called out that he was concerned for the safety of his father and had come to escort him back to Ahmar. Fatima, speaking for the Emir from the door of the plane, said that he was grateful for his solicitude but would wait for rescue in the shelter of the plane. Suleiman said he must insist. He began to threaten, and soon was offering the lives of his two hostages in return for their surrender. Clemency and Farzana were thrown forward and forced to kneel in the sand, heads bowed.

Clemency was shivering, but her mind was clear. If the Emir emerged from the plane, he would be taken away and killed. So would Fatima and Khalid. And so too would she and Farzana, because there could be no witnesses. The plane would be found, and it would be assumed – or accepted, by those who guessed the truth but preferred to reach an accord with Ahmar's new ruler – that they had set out to look for help and become lost in the desert wastes.

If they stayed in the plane, then it would be the same fate. The first of Suleiman's men to climb through the cabin door might be killed, but after that it would be a slaughter; an old man, a woman and a boy against five armed men. Or perhaps they would sit outside and spend the day shooting through the thin hull of the plane until the three of them were dead.

'Uncle Suleiman.' Khalid was standing in the doorway, small and solemn. 'Why do you force these women to kneel as if for execution? They have done you no harm.'

'They are working for my father's enemies,' he

replied. 'It would seem they have confused my father about who are his true friends.'

'If there is confusion, then should we not wait for the rescuers to come, Uncle Suleiman? Before any mistakes that cannot be made good?'

Even in the depths of her own fear, she admired his small act of defiance. Perhaps they would not trust Suleiman, after all. If they were to die in the plane, its fuselage riddled with bullet holes, at least the evidence of his treachery could not be hidden.

'You should show more respect for your elders,' Suleiman said.

'So should all true believers.'

Suleiman growled something under his breath and turned away. There was movement behind her, and then Suleiman was back, and another man stood before her. In one hand, its point resting on the sand, was a long curved sword.

'I am come to cleanse the land of Ahmar of the infidel,' Suleiman called out, speaking now to his followers as much as to the Emir and his family. 'You must hand Ahmar to me for this Holy work to be done. I will start this hour with these two devils. See, they are even dressed for their own execution.'

At her side, Farzana was sobbing. Clemency's tears were silent, because there was no escape now for her; or for Suleiman. Having made the threat, he could not back down now. To be defied by Khalid, only a child, would make him look ridiculous.

'I will come and speak to you.' Khalid called out, as if he were the Emir. He turned and spoke to someone out of sight in the shadows of the cabin, then dropped down onto the sand and came confidently to stand before his uncle.

'You must release these women, Uncle Suleiman. I command it.'

'You?'

'Last night, the blessed Emir Rashid bin Salah bin Wassan named me before witnesses as his Crown Prince. This morning, he passed on to heaven. I am now the Emir of Ahmar.'

It was a proclamation, spoken in a high, clear voice, and it rang out like the truth. At once, Suleiman turned to his men.

'This is nonsense. He lies. The Emir is still alive, and I am his named successor.'

But the men look uncertain, anxious. Khalid ignored him and called out to them.

'My first act as Emir is to command you all to go in peace back to my land. I will return there with the Emir's mortal remains and all infidelity will be forgiven.'

'He is only a child. Seize him.'

The men looked at each other, none willing to be the first to lay hands on him. After a moment, Suleiman cursed them and strode forward. He caught Khalid by the arm and swung him around. With his other hand he drew out his knife.

Khalid struggled, trying to pull away. Then Suleiman grunted and doubled over, cursing. Khalid shook himself free and turned to watch as his uncle fell to the ground. Khalid's face was a sickly colour. In his hand was a knife, stained with blood.

There was a moment when all hung in the air; the silence after an explosion. Then Khalid took the moment into his own hands. He pointed at Clemency.

'You, woman, tend to his wound. And you,' he added, pointing to the man still holding the sword. 'I wish to give you the honour to ride to Ahmar to bring news of the new Emir. I wish you to tell my Council that I will hear their advice and wisdom in the days and months to come. I will be guided by them in all things.'

Clemency was already leaning over Suleiman, but there was nothing she could do. The knife had struck him in the heart and his blood had flowed through his robes to stain the sand the darkest red. His eyes were open in surprise. Farzana leaned over and closed them.

They kept their places over Suleiman's body while Khalid took command, and sent off the messenger, and instructed the men to put fuel on the fire, prepare some food, and make a bier for the Emir's body. Then he came and looked down on the man he had killed.

'I had no choice,' he said. For a moment, he looked very young. Then his new authority returned.

'You must both go into the plane and stay out of sight. These men are now mine to command, but they are very devout and your presence will trouble them. I do not want trouble. Do you understand?'

They nodded, rose and walked slowly to the plane. Climbing inside, they saw the Emir's body laid out on the day bed, with Fatima kneeling at its side.

'The men will wish to see him,' she said, standing. 'My son is right. You must stay away.'

So they waited in the cockpit, looking out over the distant hills, as the sun rose higher, and the men came and went outside, and they began to believe that Khalid had their loyalty, and the danger was over.

Yet it was a relief when they saw a helicopter approaching, its engine harsh after the silence of the desert. It settled a few yards from the nose of the plane and they could see the Jordanian flag on its side. A man in uniform stepped down and Khalid went to greet him, and they spoke urgently for some minutes, their voices drowned by the helicopter.

They walked out of sight. Then Khalid was at the cockpit door.

'The helicopter can only take two people. You will fly with them now. Then they will return.'

Already Khalid was becoming used to issuing commands.

'It will be easier perhaps if you leave through the window,' he added. 'I am sorry we part this way, and like my father I will always be in your debt. But this is not your place now.'

Clemency opened the emergency window as wide as it would go and squirmed through, then dropped onto the ground. She turned to help Farzana, but she waved her away and jumped down beside her. The officer from the helicopter was waiting and helped them into their seats and strapped them in, and before they were even aware of it they were rising in the air, as smoothly as in a lift. The helicopter began to swing away to the east and Clemency had a last glimpse of the plane, a startling red against the muted browns of the desert, and the brunt patch of the fire, and the body of Suleiman, lying ignored while the men prepared their meal and readied their camels for the journey back to Ahmar.

# 28

They met for the last time in the flat overlooking the sea. There were five men ranged around the sofas, listening intently as she told her story. Vaughn had flown out overnight from London, along with Philip Martin from the Foreign Office, and Major Hereward was up from Ahmar. Denholm had brought her across from the Lebanese Ministry of Security, and sat at her side, as if he were her lawyer, ready to intervene if she incriminated herself. Beyond them were the windows onto the balcony, and the perfect blue of the sky.

Denholm had warned her that they had yet to decide if this were a triumph or a disaster. As she finished, neither Vaughn nor Farringdon said anything, as if unsure whether to take the lead and the responsibility that might go with it.

In the end, Major Hereward was the first to speak.

'So it was the Communists after all, stirring up these religious types. It's a damn good thing it didn't come off. Our position in Ahmar might have become untenable.'

'Instead, we have the boy Khalid,' Farringdon said. 'Do you know him?'

'A little. There's to be a Council of Five to govern on his behalf. Two of the elders, his uncles and his mother.'

There was more of this, a kind of Oxbridge seminar in which the men discussed the political fallout as if it were medieval theology.

'For the longer term,' Martin said judiciously, 'the concern is that this opens up Ahmar to Iranian influence. Particularly with Fatima as Queen Mother. It'll unsettle the Trucial states. Part of the *quid pro quo* for us being there is that we keep the Persians at arm's length. But I think we can conclude – tentatively at this stage, of course – that this is a much better outcome than had Suleiman's plan not misfired.'

Misfired; the word was so lacking in emotion or power that it was hard to link it to the bloody shambles in the cabin of Zebra Peter.

'We're clear that Suleiman is dead?' Farringdon asked generally; but all eyes turned to Clemency.

'When I left they were preparing the body for burial.'

'You're sure the other stewardess was from SAVAK?' Vaughn asked.

'It might have been their customs service. She was there to try to identify this smuggling channel but when they picked up the same information as you did about the plot, she was told to go after that.'

'That's another question,' Farringdon said. 'What do we do about Rossiter?'

'Do we need to do anything? Martin asked. 'There's no actual proof that he knew about the drug shipments.'

'Yes,' Vaughn said. 'We need to go carefully with Rossiter. He's done us a few favours over the years, and of course he has some knowledge of this operation. If we turn him in to the police or Interpol or whoever, then it might come back to bite us.'

There were a couple of nods of agreement, and Clemency realised that they were inching their way towards deciding to let Rossiter go free. She leaned forward to protest, only for Denholm to touch her lightly on the arm.

'I'm wondering how much we need to involve London in this,' Martin said. 'After all, the Air Ministry has as an interest, and the Home Office of course.'

'And the Ministry of Defence, if this stuff has been passing through the SBA in Cyprus.'

'But my point is that we don't know that it has.'

'There's also the security aspect to consider.'

Denholm interrupted them.

'It may be too late. I've heard that the *Sûreté* are preparing a warrant for his arrest. They have the evidence from the plane, you see.'

The voices were silent. She could hear them thinking; let things take their course; it was out of their hands; Rossiter would have to take his chances. They could always tell him that, if he kept the British angle out of it, they would do what they could to soften the blow with the Lebanese.

'What about the Communist connection?'

Hereward leaned forward.

'The Agency have some intel about a Soviet trawler off Sharma on the west coast of Saudi. It's likely that's how the GRU contingent were exfiltrated.'

So Petrov was on his way home. Clemency's final hopes that he might in some way be caught up in the aftermath of the plot were gone. The meeting room seemed to fade, and the blue sky beyond filled her mind. She supposed it was time to go home.

She tried to imagine the flight to London, rainy, green England, the train from Reading, and her family in the Old Vicarage, making jam and taking the dog for a walk and asking her when she was going to settle down. But it was impossible.

All that came to mind was Bill Macquarie; but she wouldn't think of that.

*

Denholm drove her out to the airport himself; as if anxious to see her safely on her way. She insisted that he shouldn't wait, so he went with her as far as the ticket desk, and once she had dropped off her bag, it was time to part.

'Well, there we are,' he said awkwardly.

'Thank you for looking after me.'

'Don't thank me. I'm just glad I can put you on this plane in one piece. I never met the friend of yours – the one who was murdered – but I can't stop thinking about her. There's so much evil in the world, Clemency, and whatever one does, it never seems enough.'

Every time she saw Denholm, it was harder to understand how it was he was an officer in SIS. Surely every report must condemn him as too emotional, lacking in the edge of steel the job demanded. And yet he was the one who had seen Suleiman as the most likely link to the Soviets. He had secured the cooperation of the Lebanese authorities. Unlike Vaughn and the others, he showed he cared, and people responded, and trusted him.

'Please don't change,' she said. 'You're the only thing here I'll miss.'

'That and the beach?'

'Yes, the beach,' she said. 'And the food. And some of the people. And the sun. Definitely the sun.

I'm not looking forward to London in December.'

She left him standing looking careworn, on the edge of chasing after her to give her one last piece of advice, and then went through to the departure lounge. On the board, she saw that the BOAC flight was delayed. She imagined the disruption this would be causing behind the neat check-in desks, the hurrying and improvisation and snappish conversations; and was pleased that it was no longer anything to do with her.

There was a row of telephone cabins to one side of the information desk. She rested her handbag and overnight bag by her feet and pulled out a handful of coins. In a moment, the operator had connected her, and a woman's voice had answered in French.

'I would like to speak to Monsieur Haddad.'

The secretary was too discreet to ask why she was calling, and in a few moments more she was put through to Gemal.

'I have the information you asked for,' Clemency said without any introduction. It was possible his phone was being tapped. 'The name is Alec Rossiter. I think you may already know him.'

'I do. And thank you.' If Gemal was surprised by the call, it didn't show. 'How confident are you that this is the man with whom I should do business?'

Clemency thought of what Farzana had told her about Rossiter, and how Petrov had not recognised her in the desert because he had no idea she was involved. Only Rossiter had an interest in liquidating her. Warning off David had been a start, but she was getting close to exposing the drug-smuggling route. Felicity had been killed by accident, but it still amounted to murder.

'I am very confident. Completely confident.'

'Good. Very good. I will, er, put the proposition to him very soon.'

They both fell silent. There was nothing left to say. Gemal might choose to forget his pledge. The attempt might fail. Or in a few days or weeks, she would read in the paper about the untimely death of a British airline executive, killed in a car crash or in a robbery gone wrong. Whatever happened, Clemency had done what she could. After a moment, she placed the receiver back in its holder and stepped out of the kiosk.

Then she felt a hand on her arm. She swung round, her hand to her mouth, to see Farzana smiling at her.

'You frightened me,' she said. 'What are you doing here?'

'The same as you. Waiting for a plane. I thought that we— '

An announcement broke in on them.

*'Will passengers for Iran Air flight 502 please go at once to Gate 7...'*

'That is my flight. So, then just goodbye. Until we meet again.'

'That isn't likely, is it? I don't even know your real name.'

'No. But you are Clemency White of the Old Rectory, Wood Stanton, Somerset. I even know the name of your dogs. If we ever need your help, I will find you.'

'How did— ' But the answer was in her bag; the letter from her brother tucked into her book to mark her page.

'That is not in my report,' Farzana said. 'Only in my head. So that we are square, my name is Farzana

Sitarian. If you are ever in Ashtan, I trust you will look for my family home and they will make you welcome.'

She hugged Clemency, and when she stood back her eyes were glistening.

'There is something else I have for you. The man in the desert. The Russian. As I think you know, his name is Anton Petrov. He is of some special interest to you?'

'He is.'

'Then I will tell you this also. There is a new unit set up. It is based in a clinic in the south of the Soviet Union, in the mountains above Stepanakert, close to our border. It reports to Petrov. We are very interested in what it might mean. So we have an agent. She says there is an Englishman there.'

Clemency felt flushed, a little sick, daring not to hope. But it had to be Peter.

'What else do you know?'

'Nothing. Even if I knew more, I could not tell you. But now you know enough to ask your people to ask mine to tell you more.'

Farzana's gaze showed both pleasure at a gift so well-received and compassion for the suffering that Clemency could not help showing.

*'This is the final call for Iran Air flight 502. Will all remaining passangers…'*

Impulsively, she took Clemency in her arms and kissed her on both cheeks.

*'Khodâ negahdâr.'*

For a long time after she had gone, Clemency gazed unseeing along the length of the departure hall. Peter was alive. It was no longer belief, or mere stubbornness. This unknown agent had seen him. And she had a place. Stepanakert. All she wanted was to find an atlas and see the word on the printed page, proof that it existed.

Farzana had hinted there might be more to learn. There was even the encouragement of his being near the border with Iran. How near? Of course, it made no real difference. He would only be recovered by negotiation and exchange. But for the first time in over a year there was something definite to go on. Even Swan couldn't ignore this.

Yet with hope came a new fear. If next week, or next month, Peter were to be freed, what then? What would he find waiting for him? Not the same Clemency White that he had left behind on a mountainside in France. She could still feel the knife sliding between the boy's ribs, and hear the breath hissing over his teeth; and then stabbing again and again, the blood flowing hot through the folds of his robe. She had killed him, buried him in the desert. She could never be the same again.

And did she want to be different? That night, watching the flames of the fire, under the stars, it had been an exquisite pleasure to be alive. The fear and the exhilaration of survival, landing the plane, even kneeling to be executed; it was a more powerful drug than anything that Stannard carried in the hold of the plane. If Swan or Vaughn asked her to go on another mission, she would be helpless, like any addict. This was her life; no, this was *her*, now. The thought sickened her. But there was no way back.

With a jolt, she heard her own flight being called. She hurried across the terminal to the check-in.

The flight attendant took Clemency's boarding pass, glanced at it and handed it back with a bright smile.

'Enjoy your flight, Miss Green.'

But Miss Green hardly seemed to hear, and her face was grey beneath her tan. *Poor thing,* the stewardess thought. *Probably scared of flying.*

THE END

Clemency White will return in
*Shadow of a Girl*